S.W.A.L.K.

by

Marion Joy

Enjoy the Journey

Regards

Marion Joy

ARTHUR H. STOCKWELL LTD
Torrs Park, Ilfracombe, Devon, EX34 8BA
Established 1898
www.ahstockwell.co.uk

British Library Cataloguing-in-Publication Data.
A catalogue record for this book is available
from the British Library.

Inspired by a true story, ship life and real situations. The names, characters
and events are the authors imaginative flair from her own experiences of
working in the cruise ship industry.
The names of the characters bear no resemblance to persons living or dead.
All rights reserved.

ISBN 978-0-7223-4919-9
Printed in Great Britain by
Arthur H. Stockwell Ltd
Torrs Park   Ilfracombe
Devon

DEDICATION

To cruise personnel all over the world, past, present and future, whose hard work, dedication and professionalism give passengers on cruise-ship holidays the most wonderful experiences and memories that last.

THE WORLD IS ROUND

Oceans, mountains, rivers,
Countries of vast lands, many peoples, many hands.
Taking a step at a time to travel far.
Blazing sunsets, sparkling stars,
Forest stretching further than the eye can see.
Temples, churches, colourful lanterns,
Azure seas. Silver sands.
And yet our planet is so small,
The huge round ball.

Come; take my hand, hold the gold bracelet band.
Don't lose touch, for it means so much.
A letter from home
Sealed With A Loving Kiss.

by

Marion Joy
August 2019

ACKNOWLEDGEMENTS

Thanks to my husband, Robert, my siblings and family. With their patience, love, kindness and understanding contributed to the writing of *S.W.A.L.K.*

Thanks to the artist, Neil Prior, a school friend, who took such great care to create the front cover from the author's specifications, using original oil on canvas. His detailed perceptive edge regarding the subject matter has created a genius cover for *S.W.A.L.K.* that stands out on the bookshelf – a cover to complement the genre and the author's unique work.

Thanks also to Arthur H. Stockwell Ltd, the publisher, for their belief, patience and diligence in the publication and circulation of *S.W.A.L.K.*

ITINERARY

The Journey

Christchurch, Dorset to London Heathrow Airport, UK.
London Heathrow Airport, UK to Miami Airport, USA.
Miami Florida, Haliday Inn to San Juan to board **MS *Spring Sun*** cruise ship.

Caribbean Cruising Itinerary

Barbados, St Thomas, Martinique, Palm Island and San Juan (home port).
Three week cruise of the west coast of America. Ports – Panama Canal to San José, Acapulco, Los Angeles, San Francisco and Vancouver, BC.

Alaskan Cruising Itinerary

Vancouver, Juneau, Ketchikan, Glacier Bay and Vancouver, BC (home port).

Three Week Caribbean Cruise on MS *Spring Sun*

Barbados, St Thomas, Martinique, Curaçoa, Palm Island, and San Juan (home port).
San Juan to Miami, USA.
Miami Airport, USA to London Gatwick, UK.
London Gatwick, UK to New Romney, East Kent.

INDEX OF CHAPTERS

The Story of the Novel S.W.A.L.K.   7

1. Partings   13
2. New Beginnings   31
3. Joining the **MS** *Spring Sun*   36
4. Introductions   40
5. "Goodbye, Cherie"   55
6. Life at Sea and the Salon   59
7. Caribbean Romantic Adventures   66
8. The Boat Race – June 1985   72
9. The Panama Run   75
10. Acapulco   79
11. Los Angeles: The City of the Famous   83
12. I Left My Heart in San Francisco   91
13. Vancouver, BC: The Dry-Dock Holiday   96
14. Alaskan Adventures   107
15. Christmas at Sea, 1985   113
16. The Homecoming   116

THE STORY OF THE NOVEL S.W.A.L.K.

S.W.A.L.K. – Sealed with a Loving Kiss – is set in a time when the world seemed so much bigger, the 1980s, before people could communicate through today's technological devices, before the Internet. It was a time for living in the moment.

Dreams, adventures, friendships and loves are born through people's perceptions and their longing for change.

On a cruise ship fun, laughter and song were the highlights of each day – being in a different place, seeing new places and landmarks, the wildlife and famous people.

Letters received from home and letters sent to loved ones were the most important communication. Telephone calls from port were rare because of the expense.

S.W.A.L.K. is about two people who meet while working at sea on the same ship. Their job roles are diverse, the ship becomes their home and they take every chance they have, away from their work, to enjoy destinations, times shared and being together.

The other people on board are their extended family, a community all of its own.

CHAPTER 1

Partings

December 1984 – Jodie was up at 5 a.m. She washed and dressed, taking great care to pay attention to detail. She wore a navy skirt suit with a white silk shirt and black three-inch stiletto heels, which she matched with a black patent clutch bag. Keeping the jewellery simple, she wore stud earrings, a silver cross chain, which looked neat around her neckline, and a pearl brooch pinned to her right lapel.

She had done her hair the night before. It was thick, strong brunette in colour, needing a light brush into place. For her make-up she had only soft beiges, mascara and soft heather-coloured lipstick, looking minimal, but as smart as possible.

This interview with Creatif-Perfection Transocean Ltd was so very important. She had, since starting her career as a hairdresser, dreamed of working at sea; a love of the ocean and the glamorous lifestyle that magazines portrayed appealed to her.

Nervously excited, she picked up her folder with all the necessary letters and documents, including her certificates and passport, then made her way downstairs to the hall. Checking for keys, her coach ticket to hand, she sat to wait for the taxi. The coach was due to leave London Victoria at 6.15 a.m.; her interview was at 10 a.m.

She had plenty of time. She made tea and toast. It was very cold in the house at 19 Endfelt Avenue. There was only a coal fire and night storage heaters. She shivered as she sipped her tea; the cup warmed her hands. Jodie had packed her leather gloves, should she need them.

Her overcoat was a woollen red ankle-length number, with a slight slit in it and padded shoulders; and double-breasted with a fur collar. She pulled it around herself. Looking up at the clock in the lounge, it said 6 a.m. She heard the engine of a waiting car outside, peeking through the net curtain, she checked it was her taxi. Jodie picked up her belongings, buttoned her overcoat, put on her gloves and opened the front door; closing it carefully so as not to disturb her parents or the neighbours.

Jodie walked towards the waiting car, carefully she opened the green gates at the end of the driveway, then clinked them shut as she looked back at the house; she then walked to the waiting taxi.

The taxi driver greeted her: "Hi, love. My name is Paul."

She replied, "Hi. I'm Jodie, my coach leaves Bar Gates at 6.15."

"Plenty of time."

"Thank you. Yes."

The coach pulled in ahead of the taxi just as they approached the meeting point, and was waiting for passengers. From what Jodie could see, it didn't look very full.

She paid the taxi driver £5, and said, "Thank you, Paul."

He wound down his window just as she was about to walk away and said, "You all right, love?"

"Yes," said Jodie. "I am sure they will look after me."

"You take care, young lady."

"I will."

Jodie waved goodbye.

The coach was waiting to go; the driver stood in the bus shelter having a cigarette; Jodie approached him.

"Is this the coach to London Victoria?" she asked.

"Yes, it is. Welcome aboard and take a seat; it's warmer at the back by the engine. My, there's a sharp frost on the ground this morning."

"Yes, there is," said Jodie. "Thank you."

She settled down in a seat midway on the lower deck, for the coach was a double-decker. The passengers next to board were for Southampton, then Basingstoke.

Jodie was conscious of travelling alone, however, she managed to sleep most of the way. It was very quiet except for the steady drone of the engine.

Three hours later they pulled into the coach station at Victoria. It was a dull place – a few benches, a toilet and about six coaches with their drivers standing by the side of them. Jodie got off the coach, thanked the driver, and made her way to a small kiosk serving as a drinks stand. A woman with a blue pinny, scruffy, scraped-back hair and loud make-up stood behind the counter, pouring tea, singing to herself.

The woman said a polite "Morning, ducks!" as Jodie walked past the stand.

Jodie turned her head and said "Hello," then carried on walking.

She had her street map with her that Ross had given her, but not quite knowing the way, she asked the tea lady, "Which way to the Tube station to go to Benbridge Street?"

The woman in the pinny eyed Jodie with a warm smile. "Walk straight on, turn right, then follow the signs for the Circle Line. You'll need a ticket – cost you £1. Takes about twenty minutes, then a short walk. Good luck, ducks. Hope you get the job!"

"Thanks. How did you know I'm going to an interview?"

"Makes sense – must be important, a young girl travelling on her own this time of day!"

Jodie smiled then. "Yes, it's an interview to travel and work."

After following the tea lady's instructions, Jodie popped out into the open air. Benbridge Street was a block away. The time was now 9.35 a.m. She hoped to be early.

11

Reaching the offices, the brass plaque on the wall outside said in bold engraved letters:

'CREATIF-PERFECTION TRANSOCEAN LTD
3rd Floor'.

Jodie entered the building, a man was sitting at a desk, smartly dressed in a navy-blue suit, with a pale-blue tie. On his lapel was a tiny anchor pin. By now her heart was pounding, her resolve to impress and get this job to travel and work on the ships made her immensely determined.

Approaching the desk, Jodie pulled herself up to look as tall as she could, though she was only five feet two inches in heels.

With a clear authoritative voice she spoke to the suited man: "I'm looking for the Creatif-Perfection Transocean offices."

The man gave Jodie a wide smile, leant over, pointing to the right of the desk.

"Follow the signs to the lift in the corridor, and then take the lift to the third floor."

She got in the lift, which stopped and set down with a ping. The door slid open. Then, directly opposite Jodie, she could see as she stepped out a picture of a model from the latest trend-setting advertisement in the *Vignette* magazine, the model had blonde short hair, shimmering skin and beautifully made-up eyes.

Noticing another desk with a young receptionist sitting at it, she walked over to see her. She looked up and smiled at Jodie, who waited patiently for her to put the phone down.

"Hello. My name is Jodie Hayes – I'm here for an interview with a Miss Chandler."

"Just a moment – let me take a look in the book. Yes, 10 a.m. You are fifteen minutes early. Take a seat and I will let her know you are here. Would you like a cup of tea?"

"Thank you. Yes, I would, please."

The young lady walked around the desk then entered a door.

Jodie took off her coat, smoothed her hair once, then sat down. She took out her mirror from her bag to check her lipstick. Her complexion was a little flushed through walking in the cold then coming into a warm office.

The receptionist appeared again with a teacup and saucer in her hand, offering it to Jodie. She took it from her.

"Thank you. I'm a bit nervous."

"You will be fine. Love your red coat. I've told Miss Chandler you are here."

Jodie sipped the warm tea and took a slow, deep breath. She took out her folder with the documents she had been asked for, to check they were all in order.

The receptionist appeared.

"Miss Chandler will see you now, if you would like to follow me."

Jodie got up, put down her cup, picked up her coat and folder then followed the girl along the corridor; her heart pounding once again. She took another deep breath.

The girl opened a door, then introduced Jodie to Miss Chandler. She was, Jodie thought, about twenty-five years old; she noted no rings. Her blonde hair was arranged in a smart low chignon. She wore a grey skirt suit, white blouse and black high-heeled shoes, make-up immaculate.

"Good morning, Jodie, please have a seat. Your interview today will be approximately one hour. I will explain to you how Creatif-Perfection Transocean operates, then a little about the job you applied for – life at sea – and the criteria we expect all our staff to meet. Then I will ask questions about your skills, and how you would respond to clients."

Jodie sat up straight, her hands in her lap, and listened intently; she answered all the questions in detail and hoped that she gave the correct answers.

Watching Miss Chandler's expressions, Jodie could not tell if she liked her or not. Every now and then Miss Chandler would stop talking to see if Jodie was listening, then would carry on.

She asked Jodie, "Why do you want to work on a cruise ship as a hairdresser?"

Jodie answered without hesitation, "It is something I have wanted to do since I was very young, to meet people from all over the world; I love hairdressing and I want to travel."

Miss Chandler took out Jodie's papers, scrutinised her certificates, then her passport, before handing them back to Jodie. Standing up, she then put out her hand for Jodie to shake, indicating the interview was over.

"Thank you, Miss Hayes, for attending today; we will be in touch by letter in due course if we think you are suitable."

Jodie replied, "Thank you, it has been very interesting." Jodie smiled. 'Was that really an hour?' she wondered to herself.

Jodie walked through to the receptionist and said a cool goodbye to her, made her way to the lift and out again from the office on to the pavement. The cold December air bit into Jodie's face. Then she made her way towards the coach station to go home to Christchurch, Dorset.

A week later Jodie came home after a busy day at the salon in Bournemouth, it was December and nearly Christmas. She walked in to find her mum smiling, sitting by the open fire in the lounge. Jodie took off her coat, gloves, hat and shoes in the hallway, then went in to warm her hands.

"Hello, Jodie. How was your day?" asked her mum.

"Fine, Mum – getting busy for Christmas, only ten days away."

"There's a letter for you, Jodie, it's on the dining-room table."

Jodie went into the dining room, she picked up the letter. It was stamped 'London'. She opened it nervously.

Dear Jodie,

We have pleasure in offering you a position of hairstylist aboard the MS Spring Sun.

You will need to come to London to get your visas and seaman's pass, go for a medical in Harley Street and process documents at the offices. Instructions will follow by letter, giving a time to attend.

Your appointment will start on 5 April 1985. Once all documents are dealt with, you will receive your flight details, itinerary, uniform and contact details of the manager in Miami, USA.

Transport to London Heathrow will be your responsibility.

We look forward to hearing from you,

Yours faithfully,

Miss Chandler

HR co-ordinator, Creatif-Perfection Transocean Ltd.

Jodie read the letter again then went into the lounge. Her dad had come in at that point with some coal for the fire.

"Hello, Jodie," he said, smiling.

He put down the coal bucket and came over to hug her.

"Dad, I got the job with Creatif-Perfection Transocean Ltd," she said, smiling, trying to hold back the emotions of joy and elation. "I'm going to America!"

"Well done, Jodie. That's fabulous news. When will you be leaving?"

"April the 5th next year."

"Not long, then, it'll be an extra-special Christmas this year?"

"Yes, it will." She gave him another hug.

Fred thought to himself of all his children, Jodie was not exactly more special than the other five, but she was much more like her mum. She had a quality of her own, a special warmth and intuition. She deserved this break – an adventure and a chance at a better future. He would sorely miss her, though – she could always brighten his day.

Jodie hugged her mum. "I'm so excited, Mum. It's so amazing."

Her mum smiled at Jodie. "I'm so pleased for you, Jodie. I'll put the kettle on – make us all a brew."

Jodie sat down opposite her dad, he started coughing.

"Dad, are you feeling OK?" she asked.

"It's nothing, Jodie – just a cough."

It would be hard leaving them, but at least they had her brothers and sisters.

The TV was on; Mum came in with a tea tray.

"Here we are, then, make some space on the table, Jodie, please."

Jodie did as she was asked, then her mum put down the tray laden with teapot, cups, saucers and Madeira cake with napkins.

Tea by an open fire at home was so much a part of everyday life in the Hayes household. Anytime anyone came over there would be a homely welcome, smiles, laughter and lots of chatting over all kinds of things. People leaving always looked forward to the next visit.

Christmas 1984

All the family came around to Christmas Day dinner, Mum got stressed, as always, and worried about the turkey being cooked in time. The boys, Dad, Jodie and Ginny went out to the Fair Mile Inn to celebrate, then were back late to meet Mum's wrath.

"Dinner is nearly cold!"

Jodie went over to her mum and hugged her tightly. "It's OK, Mum – it will be lovely. We're all here now – so let's enjoy!"

Mum calmed down, then gave Jodie a huge smile. "Yes, you're right. It's Christmas."

"Mum, we will all sit down and pass the food around. Ross, Ginny and I will wash up afterwards while you put your feet up."

The Christmas lunch was fabulous – lots of turkey and stuffing, with bread sauce, Brussel sprouts and roast potatoes; followed by the lighting of the Christmas pudding. Everyone was looking for the sixpences, buried inside it. The crackers were pulled, bad jokes told, hats put on and more alcohol poured. The meal was so filling they felt unable to move.

After Christmas lunch was cleared, they all moved into the lounge. The lights dazzled on the Christmas tree. Dad acted as Santa, passing round the presents, arranged in piles by name. Jodie's pile was an array of gifts for her trip: the latest disc camera, from Ross; a writing set with a beautiful engraved ballpoint pen, from Ginny; $50, from Deacon; a passport holder, from Caroline and a floral sarong, from her mum and dad. She felt so emotional and overwhelmed with love for all her siblings, Mum and Dad.

"WOW!" said Jodie. "Thank you so much!"

After all of the presents had been handed out to everyone, the Queen's speech came on the TV at 3 p.m. The Queen gave her message and wished all her subjects a happy New Year, 1985. Standing up, they all held a glass of sherry in their hands and toasted the Queen on the TV and sang the national anthem.

More food from the buffet spread in the evening. When other relations came – Caroline and her husband, Percy, arrived with the children; Ivan and Luke, bearing yet more gifts. Then Ken, Ross, Ginny, Mum, Dad and

Jodie set up the cards around the cleared table at nine-ish for a long game of Newmarket. Playing with just pennies, any pennies earned, were put back in the pot for next year.

More drinks flowed, silly jokes told, happy memories shared and music played. Such a happy easy time was had by all; it was indeed a special Christmas.

January 1985

January came around after a superb New Year's Eve pub crawl, around Christchurch town's ten pubs, for Jodie and her friends.

Jodie handed in her notice at the end of January, at The Upper Cut Hair Salon. The owner, Mrs Trim, was gracious, she said she hoped the job at sea would be everything Jodie expected it to be. Jodie was glad Mrs Trim was all right about her notice and plans for moving on.

Jodie took her holiday in February, then spent the next weeks organising what to take for her trip to the London offices. The company had booked her into the Hotel Montrise in Benbridge Street, to be nearby.

Jodie made her way up to London very early again on 14 February, on the 6 p.m. coach. Her appointment in Harley Street was at 10 a.m., then the American Embassy at 12 noon and the offices at 2 p.m. Eventually Jodie got to the Hotel Montrise, had dinner then sank into bed, exhausted.

Making her way home the next day, which was Saturday, it all seemed so unreal, like a dream. Her excitement was obvious. When chatting to friends, Jodie could only think of being at sea and working on the **MS *Spring Sun***.

Jodie was worried about her dad, though, his health wasn't good. The Doctor had called several times and he diagnosed acute pneumonia. Mum was nursing him, but he refused to go into hospital. He didn't want to leave her. They were so close. He looked tired and physically exhausted.

Jodie became unsure about her decision to take the job.

February 1985

The end of February came around, Jodie was at work. It was a Friday, a busy day, in the salon the phone rang, Mrs Trim answered it.

"Good morning. Can I help you . . . ? Yes, I will get her for you, Caroline."

As Jodie was about to wash her next client's hair, Mrs Trim interrupted her, saying there was a call from home.

Jodie went to reception taking the phone from Mrs Trim.

"Hello, Caroline."

"Jodie, you will need to come home. It's Dad," she said, her voice strained.

"What's happened, Caroline?"

"He died of a massive heart attack about an hour ago. Ken's with Mum; Ginny's on her way. I've telephoned Deacon and Ross, but they are not home, I'll keep trying."

Jodie was speechless, her worst fears had been realised: she had lost her lovely dad.

She managed a "Yes, I understand, Caroline. I will come as soon as I can."

She spoke quietly to Mrs Trim: "I have to go home."

"Yes, of course – your family need you, Jodie."

Jodie's head was in a daze, but as she walked her calmer side kicked in, she picked up her coat, gloves and scarf, found her car keys from her handbag, then crossed the road to where her car was parked. A blue Mini. Somehow she started the engine, and on automatic pilot, she made her way from Boscombe centre to home, and Endfelt Avenue.

Pulling up outside home. The gates were open, with

Ken's, Ross's and Caroline's cars parked inside the driveway. The curtains were closed. Jodie opened the front door to be greeted by Ginny, who had clearly been crying, her eyes a bloodshot red.

Ginny put her arms around Jodie. "Where's Mum, Ginny?" asked Jodie.

"She's upstairs having a lie-down, the Doctor's on his way. Dad's in the lounge, we've called the undertaker."

"OK, Ginny, I'm going up to see Mum."

Jodie made her way upstairs to comfort her mum, she was sleeping. Jodie approached the bed where her mum was lying down.

Quietly she said, "Mum, I'm sorry. How are you feeling?"

"Jodie, love." Mum sat up in bed then opened her arms and gestured to Jodie to come and sit with her.

Jodie held her mum tight, then drew away and looked in to her soft-hazel eyes. "He was such a lovely man, Mum. We'll all miss him." Jodie held her mum. "I'll get you a cup of tea, Mum. You rest awhile."

"Thanks, Jodie."

"Keep warm, Mum. Would you like a hot-water bottle?"

"Yes, that will be nice, Jodie."

Jodie thought to herself how pale Mum looked.

"See you in a moment or two, Mum."

Jodie left the room, quietly making her way downstairs to the kitchen. She prepared tea and a hot-water bottle, then Ginny came into the kitchen.

"Is that for Mum?"

"Yes, it is."

"Can I take it up to her?"

"Yes, if you like, Ginny." Jodie sensed her deep sadness.

As Ginny left to go upstairs to their mum, Jodie went out into the garden, even though it was a damp, cold day. Ross saw her from the kitchen window, he went out to his younger sister.

"You OK, Jodie? You seem so calm."

He put his arm around Jodie, his youngest sister.

"Yes, Ross. I know he hadn't been well since Christmas, he was so pleased for me getting my dream job. How can I leave Mum now? She will be so lonely."

Ross was thoughtful.

"Now you listen to me, Jodie. I'm a little older than you, I have worked for the same company for twenty years and have never had the chance of trying something exciting like you are now. Take it with both hands and enjoy every minute. You are twenty-one, you have your whole life ahead of you. Mum wouldn't want to hold you back and Dad would want you to go. Besides, you need to put the camera to good use," he said with a smile.

How was it Ross, of all her siblings, could always cheer her up and help calm her fears, like years ago when there was a thunderstorm? He had this wonderful way of analysing the worst situations and seeing the bright side of them. Jodie looked straight at her brother.

"Yes, you're right – I do want to go to sea, my mind's in a fog."

"We will know the date for the funeral soon, and when you leave I'll take you to Aunty Patricia's unless you need to go straight to the airport. She will be coming to the funeral. Dad was Aunty Patricia's half-brother."

"Yes, it will be good to see her."

Aunty Patricia was Jodie's favourite aunty. She was a cheerful outgoing lady who had never married and lived with her sister Lina in London. A professional, she had joined the police service at twenty-three. She was fun and loving, much like their dad.

Dad had fallen in love with Mum when he was stationed at Blandford army barracks in the Second World War. The story went that he and his mates would take the steam train to Christchurch and make their way to the Fair Mile Inn for fun, a sing-song and a few drinks. It's where he met Mum. They married in the Priory, and then stayed in Christchurch to raise their family together.

Mum was born and brought up by foster-parents while her brothers and sisters were brought up in workhouses. She always said she was the lucky one – she got to grow up on a smallholding with animals, had her own horse, chickens and even a pet rabbit. The lovely cottage Granny Joan owned was surrounded by roses. Mum took up nursing at nineteen in those days, and worked at Christchurch Hospital, dealing with wounded soldiers.

Meeting 'her Fred', as she called him, changed her life. They loved the family, living by the sea, at Christchurch, Hampshire.

Dad called her Kit for short, or Kitty, she'd been named after her mum, Kathleen, who had died two days after giving birth to her. Now Mum had lost the love of her life, and her youngest daughter was about to leave her to go to sea as a hairdresser, in just over four weeks' time.

The next few weeks flew by for Jodie, most of the time she was in a haze of emotions, varying from the sombre to the elated. Her dad was to have a cremation; it was the first funeral Jodie would attend, she and Ginny were looked after by relations when their grandfather died – they were eight and ten years old.

It came to the day of Dad's funeral and Ross had to persuade Jodie to attend.

The hearse was waiting with her siblings to follow their mum and the coffin.

"I don't want to go, Ross," she said quietly.

"You need to, Jodie," he said gently, holding her hand.

"No! He is in my heart and in my mind. My sixth sense is kicking in, Ross."

"Jodie, no one likes funerals."

Jodie saw his pain then.

"I am sorry, Ross – you need me, don't you?" she asked.

"As a matter of fact, yes, I do!" he replied.

Jodie stood up from the garden bench where she and Ross had been sitting.

"Right, let's go, then, but don't leave me alone!"

"I won't, Jodie – I'll be right beside you," he assured his younger sister.

March 1985

Sadness reigned over the Hayes household like a grey cloud. Jodie's leaving date for work came around and she started to prepare to leave for the journey that would, though she didn't know it, shape her life.

Her mum lost her smile and her appetite; her face looked pale. Caroline popped in regularly to see Mum with her children, Luke and Ivan. They cheered their grandmother, but both asked where Grandad was. Caroline, gentle with her sons, said Grandad was with the angels in heaven. Ken made time also, checking Mum was OK financially, she seemed so lost, in a complete daze.

Jodie continually worried she was doing the right thing, but in her heart she longed for adventure.

April 1985

Mum's birthday came around on 2 April. Jodie bought her a box of chocolates and flowers. The others arranged to take her to lunch at Mudeford Quay, where she and Dad loved to go walking along by the sea. She seemed cheerier that day, then turned to Jodie.

"Jodie, I will miss you. You mustn't worry about me – I have all the family to care for me, and Ginny's getting me a cat for company."

"Yes, Mum, I know, that's a great idea, it will give you something to care for."

They hugged, leant on the wall where they were walking and looked out towards the Isle of Wight, where the sun shone high in the sky on that warm spring day; the sea lapping on the shoreline.

The day soon came around for Jodie to set off on her travels. She had her luggage packed: she had bought two special cocktail dresses for formal nights, several T-shirts for the warm Caribbean weather, a few cardigans, trousers, her uniform (which was a brown skirt and checked blouse), three pairs of shoes, and her toiletries; some books, tapes of her favourite music (Michael Johnson and Paul Younger) for her Walkman, and a small clutch bag to hold her documents in.

She wore light-coloured blue jeans, a white shirt and blue sweatshirt with red pumps. As she picked up her belongings she looked around her bedroom to see if there was anything she had missed, she spotted her lucky charm, which Ginny had given her, and the disc camera – Ross's Christmas present to her. She picked them up and put them in the top of the case.

Then as she descended the stairs she could hear Ross talking to Mum. By the time Jodie had got to the bottom, Mum had gone outside. Ross was stood in the doorway and had just closed the inner glass door, he looked up at Jodie as she was struggling with her case.

"Jodie, I'll get that for you."

He took two strides, taking the case from her hand as she reached the bottom steps, she followed him to the end of the hall. Putting her arms around Ross, she gave him a hug, then kissed him on the cheek.

"I'm ready to roll. I'll just say cheerio to Mum. Where's she gone?"

"Out in the garden to get the washing in."

Jodie went to find her.

"MUM, I'm just about to leave," she hollered.

Jodie's mum came over to her youngest daughter, putting her arms around her.

"You take good care of yourself, Jodie. Don't forget to write."

"I will, Mum, you take care also. I will phone, but it is expensive and I'm not sure when I will be in port for long enough."

Jodie let go of her mum then walked out to the front gate, where Ross was just putting her luggage in his car. Jodie's mum stood in the doorway of number 19.

"I'll wave you off from here," she shouted to them.

Jodie settled herself into the front seat. Ross had the engine running.

The spring flowers were looking lovely, Jodie noted: daffodils and tulips that bobbed around in the wind. She shut the passenger door.

"Righto, young lady, let's make for Heathrow Airport. Are you meeting another person to fly out with?"

"Yes, Ross, her name is Cherie Cunningham. She's from Chester. I have a picture of her the company sent via post, our flight is at 5 p.m."

"Plenty of time, then – it's 11.50 a.m. We'll stop for a sandwich and a cuppa on the motorway."

"That will be nice, Ross, thank you."

Ross put the radio on and Jodie dozed off just after Southampton; junction 1 to the M3 for London.

Ross was an excellent driver. He stopped for twenty minutes at the service station halfway, Jodie made a visit to the Ladies. They bought a sandwich and then settled down again to join the traffic. It was a Friday – surprisingly the roads were fairly quiet.

After three hours Ross pulled in, outside Heathrow Airport Terminal 1, Arrivals and Departures, Jodie was amazed at how orderly everything was. The sound of aeroplane engines filled the air, as well as cars coming and going, and the bustle of people. It was 2.30 when they arrived – two and a half hours before take-off.

"Here we are, Jodie. We'll need to look for your friend Cherie."

Ross looked around.

Jodie got out of Ross's car, then went to stand on the pavement near the entrance. He opened the boot to take out Jodie's luggage. They walked in together to join the other waiting passengers. The ticket said 'Terminal 1'; they read the signs and followed people through.

'DEPARTURES – NO NON-PASSENGERS BEYOND THIS POINT'.

Ross stopped and turned to Jodie. "Well, this is where I leave you, Sis."

"Guess it is, Ross." She put her arms around him and hugged him tight. Jodie would miss him.

"Now, you take care of yourself and mind you write home and tell me how you're doing. Take lots of pictures."

"Yes, I will," said Jodie.

She picked up her luggage, went towards the passageway to have her passport stamped, then turned and waved to Ross, blowing him a kiss at the same time. Once he saw her through, he was gone. Jodie felt for the first time alone.

CHAPTER 2

New Beginnings

Jodie searched around the waiting passengers. Cherie was easy to spot, she was the only girl her age in the departure lounge that day, and she wore a pink jumpsuit matched with pink trainers. Then, looking up, she beamed a huge smile at Jodie, she was exactly as the office had described her: blonde-haired, warm-natured and friendly.

Cherie got up from her seat as Jodie approached, putting her handbag behind her.

"Hello, Jodie. I've been so looking forward to meeting you," she said.

Jodie was laughing. "Cherie, and I'm so glad to see you. My brother dropped me here. He's had to go and I was a little lost back there."

Cherie, laughing also, then gave Jodie a hug. "You look exactly like your picture." Cherie took out the picture she had been given of Jodie and showed her.

Jodie and Cherie sat down, then chatted as if they had been friends all their lives.

"Cherie, I've never flown before, America is such a long flight – eight hours. If we leave England at five today we get in their time at eight."

"Yes, that's about right. I do hate having to wait around. It is exciting, isn't it?"

"Yes, Cherie – a night at the Haliday Inn, MIAMI, Florida! Then the next day we join the **MS *Spring Sun*** in San Juan for the Caribbean. I can't believe how lucky we are!"

Just then the voice over the Tannoy announced, **"The flight BA 757 to Miami, Florida, is ready for boarding.**

Please have your boarding passes ready and only your hand luggage with you."

"Here we go, then," said Jodie.

"Looks like we are on our way," said Cherie.

Each collected their belongings, then joined the queue to the red tape, where a hostess was waiting to show them the way to the plane. Jodie was feeling a little scared, like a child going to school for the first day. Cherie was ahead of her.

On boarding, Cherie sat in the window seat and Jodie next to her. The plane was full. A screen was directly in front of their seats, 342 and 343. Cherie was remarkably calm, she turned to Jodie and squeezed her hand.

"You'll be fine – nothing to it."

Jodie found it hard to smile at this point. She settled into her seat, took a deep breath, buckled her seat belt and closed her eyes. She wished she had taken a travel-sickness pill.

About an hour into the flight, after the stewardess had done her safety drill, Jodie started to relax and watch the in-flight movie. Dinner was served: chicken, potatoes and vegetables, followed by chocolate pudding. The drinks available were tea, coffee, cocoa and wine.

Cherie drifted off to sleep. Jodie took out her notebook and wrote down the day's events, her mind flowing back also to her dad's funeral. He had been so pleased for Jodie. In her mind's eye she could see his face smiling back at her, his grey-blue eyes twinkling with pride.

The next thing she heard was the loudspeaker announcement: **"Please fasten your seatbelts. Put away bags. We will be landing in Miami Airport in twenty minutes. The weather in Miami is warm, balmy, with a slight wind speed."**

Jodie yawned and stretched, then the aeroplane wheels bumped the tarmac of the runway.

The MS *Spring Sun*, April 1985.

Being a Friday, the **MS *Spring Sun*** had come alongside her allocated berth in the port of San Juan to disembark passengers and turn around by 5 p.m. the next day. The ***Spring Sun*** would then sail on her Caribbean run, cruising to six Caribbean ports: Barbados, the Grenadines, Martinique, St Martin and St Thomas and San Juan – a one night stay. The weather that morning was warm, with blue skies and a slight breeze.

Turnaround day for crew was a busy day; depending on the job role on board. CPO Kalvin Wheeler and CPO Paul Chapman had been on watch since 4 a.m. and were due to finish their shifts at 8 a.m. They had seen the sunrise over the Caribbean Sea. The crossing from St Thomas had been calm, quiet and tranquil.

They were both looking forward to finishing their shifts. The plan for the day was to go ashore and head for the bar and restaurant San Amigo's, to see the England v Spain World Cup qualifying game. Although the commentating would be in Spanish, the game had been advertised to be a good one. Their next shift would start at midnight, leaving them the whole day and evening to relax.

Kalvin and Paul arranged to meet in the crew galley at 8.15 a.m. Putting their caps on the top of the galley lockers, they queued to get a cooked breakfast and an English tea.

Kalvin arrived first, then Paul five minutes later.

"All done, then, Paul? It was a great sunrise this morning," said Kalvin.

"Yes, all finished now. I'm looking forward to going ashore to see the big match."

"Let's hope England are up to the job! Got to be better than the last World Cup qualifying match!"

"Alan Sharma is a good player, great at defence. David Blithe seems a smart footie player – he's scored ten goals this season."

"Yes, they should do well."

Finally they got to the front of the queue.

"This breakfast looks great. I'm so hungry I could eat a horse, Kalvin!"

"Yep, me too," said Kalvin.

They sat in the crew galley, amongst the shop girls, who seemed just as excited about going ashore as they did. All were having their lunch out and would then go to the disco in a club later. The shops on board were always closed when in port, so their day was clear.

Kalvin spoke to Sheila, the manageress: "Hi there. If you're going ashore you're welcome to share a taxi with us. We're off to the bar San Amigo's to see the England v Spain qualifying match."

"Thanks, Kalvin, but there are six of us. I'm not sure if there's a minibus to take us all."

"Good point – too many, then?"

"Yes – sorry. Thanks for asking. The girls are really excited about a night out ashore."

Sheila said, "There's new crew arriving today. One of the hairdressers went home at the end of her contract."

"Oh, yes," said Paul, "and Mandy, the beautician. They'll probably arrive mid afternoon. The company Creatif-Perfection Transocean send their staff out together."

"Yes. I'll say hello to them, Kalvin, and drag them out to the crew bar on Monday night for the quiz."

"Great idea!" said Paul.

Kalvin and Paul finished their breakfast, got up, then put their dishes and trays in the stack.

"Righto!" said Kalvin to Paul. "I'll just go below to get my wallet and crew pass, then meet you on the lower gangway."

"Will do," said Paul. "Ten minutes?"

"No worries," said Kalvin.

CHAPTER 3

Joining the MS *Spring Sun*

Jodie and Cherie alighted from the plane on to a balmy, breezy airport. Miami Airport was a lot bigger than Jodie had imagined it to be. There were porters taking luggage on small trucks to the airport from the planes. They made their way to arrivals, and on the entrance door stood a tall policeman in a uniform of black trousers, white shirt and black cap, the badge imprinted 'MP'. The gun belt on his waist to the left, a radio to the right. Tall and imposing.

"Good day, ma'am," he said. "Please make your way to immigration."

They did as they were told and queued in line with the rest of the passengers. Then after collecting their luggage, they made their way to the exit. A porter approached the girls and offered his assistance.

"Ma'am," – he addressed Jodie – "can I help you find transport?" He looked Spanish and spoke with a Californian accent, very polite.

"Yes, please," said Jodie. "My friend and I need to get to the Haliday Inn."

"No problem, ma'am. I'll hail you a taxi!"

The porter waved his arm in the air at a taxi, which stopped just short of the girls and their luggage. The driver got out, opened his boot then came over to introduce himself.

"Hi there, ma'am. I'm Janto, at your service." He tipped his head forward.

Cherie paid the porter $5, then joined Jodie. Janto opened the boot for their luggage.

"Where are you heading?" he asked in a Spanish-American accent.

31

Jodie thought it would have helped if she could speak Spanish.

"Could you please take us to the Haliday Inn?"

"Certainly, ma'am." He opened the back seat of the yellow cab for the girls, to get in.

They passed rows of sidewalks, palm trees, more hotels, bars and traffic lights which were higher than the ones at home. Everything, to Jodie, seemed so big. They stopped after a thirty minute drive.

"Here we are, ma'am – just up this driveway," said Janto.

Jodie and Cherie were speechless; the hotel looked enormous, and right out in front was a swimming pool with a bar area. Jodie and Cherie giggled to each other.

"I wonder what the rooms are like, Jodie," commented Cherie.

Janto pulled the taxi up as near as he could to the Haliday Inn. They got out and Janto took their luggage to the front steps, which were adorned with colourful tropical plants.

Jodie turned to him: "Thank you, Janto. Here's $5 for you."

"Thank you, ma'am. You both have a good day."

Cherie and Jodie opened the door to their hotel room. Tired, hungry and with mixed emotions they put their luggage on the beds.

"Wow! Look at these beds! They are huge!"

"Queen-size – they are fabulous, Jodie."

Jodie sat on the edge and bounced up and down on hers.

"Ha ha! I've died and gone to heaven, Cherie!"

"Yes," – as she sat on hers – "it's fabulous."

Jodie stood up and looked around.

"We have a view over the pool."

"Oooh! Let's get changed and go down. I'm tired, but I

don't want to miss a minute, Jodie!"

"We're in America!" They said together.

"Ha ha! So amazing, Jodie!"

"What's the bathroom like? Let's go see, Cherie."

They opened the bathroom door, to find a double basin set in marble with gold taps, a toilet, a sink with a bidet next to it, a corner bath and separate shower. Bathrobes hung on the door, with slippers in the pockets of each robe.

Speechless, Jodie went to get her camera.

"I'm snapping this and pictures of the room. I love this new disc camera. My family bought it for me, Cherie."

"Let's get changed, Jodie, and go down to have a drink by the pool. It's so sunny out – must remember the suntan lotion."

"Great, Cherie."

They unpacked to find their bikinis and summer clothing, sandals, towels and sunglasses. Covered up with dressing gowns, then they headed to the hotel pool. As they sat on two sunloungers side by side, the waiter came over.

"May I help you?"

Jodie spoke first: "Yes, please. Two very alcoholic cocktails, please."

"May I recommend Blue Mermaid Mist, ma'am?"

"That sounds amazing – two of those, please."

He left to get the drinks.

The girls took off their shoes, put on the suntan lotion and lay out on the loungers. The palm trees gave a little shade. Noted was the lifeguard, who was easy on the eye.

"Cherie, this is heaven."

"Yes. Best make the most of it – tomorrow we join the **MS *Spring Sun*** as crew, and we are going to be very busy."

"I am so excited, Cherie, here's the waiter with our drinks."

The cocktails were as blue as the ocean, adorned with umbrellas, fruit and sugar-coated edges. He set them down on the table between them. Cherie tried hers first.

"Wow! That's got a kick to it!"

"Let's see," Jodie said as she tasted hers.

"Yes, it has! I wonder what's in it."

"Well, Jodie, we'll never know."

They giggled.

"One hour then. After that it's a shower, dinner and meet up with our boss for more instructions at 9 p.m."

Cherie fell asleep; Jodie also dozed off in the warm Miami afternoon sunshine.

CHAPTER 4

Introductions

It was Jodie's first day off at sea and she didn't intend to waste it. She got up, dressed in her bikini and a floral sarong, and then made her way to the crew sun deck. Taking her Walkman with earphones, sunscreen, a towel, a book and a pair of sunglasses.

It was a warm balmy day, a little cloudy in the Caribbean, the **Spring Sun** making her way to Barbados. Jodie wanted to work on her tan. It was so lovely to feel the warmth of the sun on her body. She found a great sunbed in a sunny but shady spot, laid out her towel, then stretched out.

Jodie loved life at sea – the salty smell of the ocean, the warm days going from port to port with the crew, the interesting passengers, not driving to work, and being part of a huge family.

It was a male-dominated world; Jodie and the girls in the salon and shops were constantly being eyed up by the guys. They learnt to be polite, ignore them if they got too close, but sometimes it could be unnerving. It felt like they were seducing you with their eyes. This afternoon was to be no exception.

Settling into her book, *Romance in the Sapphire*, Jodie, despite her headphones, heard a voice from above. Looking up, she saw a guy she had never seen before, checking the safety equipment, sitting on the steps on the deck above her. He had a rope in his hands; Jodie presumed he was tying knots with it.

"Hi, I'm Kalvin. How's your book?"

"Hi, I'm Jodie; yes, it's fine, thank you."

"A good day to be on the sun deck?"

"Yes, it is. I just want to enjoy the sun." She was abrupt. Kalvin noted she was irritated by his presence.

"OK, I just wanted to make conversation."

"Thanks – maybe later," Jodie replied.

He got up then, and walked away towards the door leading to the galley.

Jodie settled down, listening to her music through her Walkman. She had the latest Paul Younger cassette. Before she knew it, it was 5 p.m. – time to go in and get ready for a formal night.

She had just got back to her cabin, showered, and then wrapped a towel around herself when there was a knock at the door.

"Hi, Jodie. It's Cherie. How's your day been?"

"Hi, Cherie. Yes, great. I got some rays – it's just annoying when guys try to talk to you when you obviously want to sunbathe. I wondered, would you mind putting moisturiser on my back?"

"Sure thing. This one?" She indicated the white bottle labelled 'Claritons Aftersun' on the dresser.

"Yes, that's the one."

Jodie sat on the bunk sideways; Cherie sat behind her, and then applied the lotion. Jodie closed her eyes and enjoyed the soothing hands. Cherie was a fabulous therapist, Jodie felt relaxed now after a day in the sun.

"Looks like the tan's coming along, Jodie – golden-coloured."

"Mmm, that was fab, thank you."

Cherie finished off with a neck-rub.

"The guys, Cherie – they just can't help ogling! Been at sea too long."

"Well, we have only been on the **Spring Sun** a week."

"Does seem longer."

"Yes, it does. What are you wearing for the formal night?"

"I thought I might wear that new red dress and black stilettos."

"That will look great, Jodie."

"And you, Cherie? You look amazing in pink."

"Yes, I thought I would wear my pink, shiny jumpsuit and pink heels."

"Great! Well, I guess we had better get a move on – only half an hour until we have to parade."

"I'll leave you to it, Jodie."

"I'll call by, Cherie. We'll go up to the Ludo together."

"OK, Jodie." Cherie gave her friend a hug. "See you in twenty-five minutes, then."

"Will do, Cherie."

Jodie got herself ready. She gave a quick glance in the dressing-table mirror – there was no full-length mirror. Yes, she'd do. She made her way to Cherie's cabin, just along the corridor, tapped a hello and Cherie let her in.

"Wow!" said Jodie. "You look fabulous!"

Cherie had made a special effort with her make-up, sparkly eyes and her hair was just a bit wild.

Jodie grinned. "Now those eyes will burn right through us!"

Cherie laughed. "Yep, I think they will."

"Ha ha!"

"Let's go, then."

Cherie locked her cabin door, then she and Jodie made their way to the middle stairwell. It had taken them just about four days to find their way around the many passageways of the **MS Spring Sun**, finally getting the hang of it. They made their way forward, and then up three decks in the lift. As they stepped out of the lift, their salon manageress, Jayne, was talking to an officer – there was no quick escape.

"Hi, girls. I would like to introduce you to Mike, he's the second engineer."

"Hello, Mike," said Cherie and Jodie together.

Mike was six feet four, dark, handsome and smart in his dress uniform: white dinner jacket, black trousers and officer's cap. Jodie noted his shiny shoes.

"Hello, ladies." He addressed Jodie and Cherie. "Would you ladies care to join us in the officers' mess for a darts match later? After cocktail hour? We are short of players."

Jodie smiled. "Well, Mike, I guess we could help you out just this once."

Mike gave a wry smile. "And you are?" he asked.

"Jodie Hayes and Cherie Cunningham." Jodie put out her hand in offer of a handshake.

Mike took it and looked straight into Jodie's eyes. He was too sure of himself, Jodie wasn't sure she liked him.

"Well, we will see you later, then," he said curtly. "If you'll excuse me, Jayne, I have passengers to attend to."

"Yes – 8.30 p.m., the officers' mess?"

"Yes, 8.30 p.m.," he repeated.

Then he turned and strode to the dining room.

Jodie turned to Cherie: "Let's get a cocktail."

"Yes, Pina Candida and a mother's ruin – make that two. May as well make the most of cocktail hour."

"Jayne, are you joining us?"

"Thanks, yes. Make mine a non-alcoholic one."

They went to the bar, ordered drinks, then watched with fascination as the bartender made up and decorated the cocktails with umbrellas on one side and cherries on cocktail sticks on top. The girls picked up their cocktails, thanked the bartender, Alvin, and then looked for a place to sit.

"Let's sit over by the window, Cherie."

"Yes, good idea. Look – Lottie's there too and Julia."

They waved a hi.

As the passengers were making their way into the lounges for cocktail hour, the seats were filling up. Rory and the band were playing Caribbean music on the steel drums and maracas as accompaniment. Beautifully dressed ladies shimmering in elegance, their partners in full dinner suits. Photographers were on hand for the passengers to be captured on camera with the ship's senior officers, and captain.

Jodie, Cherie, Jayne, Lottie and Julia sat in their seats and soaked up the scene, slowly sipping the delightful cocktails, the fruity alcoholic flavours smoothly gliding to the back of the throat.

At eight twenty-five the passengers started disappearing to dinner. The girls decided to leave also, to change into casual evening attire for the darts match in the officers' mess.

The girls arrived below decks just as the darts match was starting at 9 p.m. There were five players on each team, to include Cherie and Jodie. Mike read them the rules, it was as well that Jodie had played darts at the holiday camp near her home with her brothers; – at least she kind of knew how to play.

They were gallantly introduced to Douglas, Michael, Julian, John, Kalvin and Paul. The teams were made up from ten people – six guys and four girls. Drinks, served from the bar, were free for visitors. Jayne had her usual gin and tonic, Cherie a Pina Candida, Lottie a glass of wine and Jodie a Bahama Mamma.

After introduction, the girls were told that the last match ended in a draw. It was essential that this one ended in a clear win as the league was at a crucial stage. The league raised monies for the British Seamen's Association and the ship's crew's Christmas fund. The winning team donated fifty per cent of the winnings. Each player paid £2 to enter.

The officers on each team let the salon girls go first in each game, of which there were six. It gave teams time to finish by 11 p.m. A waiter, Elfie, a young lad from Yorkshire with a broad accent, kept track of the scores. The scores were counted twice to check that they were accurate and no one was cheating.

Jodie was on the team with the guy that was on the sun deck sitting on the steps. She learnt his name was Kalvin Wheeler. He was a good player. Jodie pulled off a bullseye on her first shot, and their team was in the lead by the third game. She was applauded by the teams for her aim.

Jayne's, Cherie's and Lottie's aims were just as good, and by the fourth game it looked like ending in another draw, until Kalvin hit another bullseye and Jodie finished on a double 20, making their team the winners by ten points. Rounds of applause from the guys to the girls. Everyone cheered the victors, had another round of drinks then said goodnight.

As Cherie and Jodie were leaving, Kalvin followed them out.

"Jodie, you were great, well played. That last throw clinched us the win," he said.

"Thanks. My brothers taught me."

She stopped and turned to face him.

Kalvin smiled, so pleased that he had finally got to talk to her, she was so pretty, smart and different.

"I'm Kalvin, chief petty officer in charge of health and safety around the ship. I met you yesterday, you were reading your book on the sun deck."

"Yes, it was such a lovely day, I just wanted to chill."

"Can I walk you back to your cabin?"

Jodie looked at Cherie with a smile and she read Jodie's thoughts. If this guy thought he was getting a tête-à-tête with Jodie he was very much mistaken.

Cherie said to Jodie, "I'm going to get some air before going to the cabin. Want to join me?"

"Yes, great idea, Cherie. I love the sea air."

Jodie turned to Kalvin, who was waiting for an answer, or waiting to come with them.

"Thanks, Kalvin, but we will be fine."

He was disappointed, but tried not to show it.

"I may drop by the salon tomorrow for a haircut."

"OK. Best make it early before the passengers come in after breakfast."

Jodie analysed Kalvin's hair without touching it. It was fair and fairly fine, with a fringe.

"Will do," said Kalvin. "About eight forty-five?"

"Yes. Goodnight."

"Goodnight, Jodie," he said. He gave Jodie a reassuring smile, then walked away in the opposite direction.

The next day Jodie was very tired, was up a little later than usual and got to work for five to nine. She had forgotten that Kalvin was coming in for a haircut.

Several days later, a Friday, they came into the port of St Thomas. Jodie was on duty in the salon with a new therapist, Jill. Jodie was at the desk dealing with a client enquiry when Kalvin came in.

"Hello, Jodie," he said. "I'm just running checks." He took the fire-extinguisher canister off the casing and looked at the valve top and the bottom for cracks. "Looks OK," he said. He put it back. "Should be fine."

The lady having her hair done, left. Jill went to the Ladies, leaving Jodie on her own talking with Kalvin. He so wanted to get to know Jodie. She was different, he plucked up the courage – it was now or never.

He took a deep breath and said, "Jodie, I need a haircut, although I was wondering if, when we pull into port tomorrow, you would have lunch with me in San Juan – go ashore with me?"

Jodie thought for a moment, he did seem a genuinely nice guy, fairly good-looking with deep smiling eyes. He did need a haircut though and she didn't have to get involved. Maybe it would be nice to have a guy show her around the town.

"Well, Kalvin, I don't have any firm plans. Yes, that would be good."

Kalvin smiled. "OK, let's meet by the gangway, about 10 a.m."

"Sounds a good plan," agreed Jodie. "I had best give in or you will be following me all over the ship for the next eight months!"

"Great – it's a date, Jodie. Can you cut my hair?"

"Ha ha! Well, I'm not going out with a scruff. Sit down and I'll sort it out."

He did as he was told; then after she had finished he put on his cap and stood up to leave.

"It looks great. Thanks, Jodie."

Jodie smiled at him. "See you tomorrow, Kalvin."

Kalvin smiled back, so happy she had accepted his invitation, he was looking forward to tomorrow.

The **Spring Sun** got under way at 5 p.m. to sail to San Juan for turnaround day. Jodie and Jill finished work at 7 p.m. They went to get dinner in the crew galley.

"Do you fancy going out this evening?" Jill asked Jodie over dinner.

"Jill, I am pretty tired. I think I'll go catch a movie in the cinema, then fall into bed after a long shower."

"You know, Jodie, that's a great idea. We'll be in San Juan tomorrow, I'm going out with the girls. Let's do that. If you don't feel like drinking this evening, I'll get a cool glass of lemonade for both of us."

As it was the last evening of the cruise, the ship quietened down after midnight. Jodie and Jill felt the smooth rocking of the ship as it went through the water on its journey to its home port of San Juan in the Caribbean. It rocked them gently to sleep.

The next day Kalvin was up earlier than usual. He had been on watch duties from midnight to 4 a.m. After three hours' sleep, he then went to the galley for breakfast. It was a beautiful morning as the **MS *Spring Sun*** made her way into the port of San Juan. Having showered and changed into blue jeans and a short-sleeved shirt, socks and trainers, his dark tanned arms and face complementing his look, he was almost ready to meet Jodie and go ashore.

The usual organised chaos was going on with the luggage. Passengers were everywhere, waiting to disembark. He found a seat on the upper deck with a cup of tea, keeping out of the way until all was clear and the crew announcement was given over the Tannoy that the crew were clear to take their shore leave.

"All crew that have shore leave may now disembark by way of the crew gangway. Please be on board by four thirty. Sailing is at 5 p.m."

Kalvin made his way forward towards the crew gangway to wait for Jodie. She arrived at just the same time.

"OK?" he asked. "All set?"

"Yes, lead on."

"Ladies first, Jodie."

As he stepped aside for her to go down the steps, the officer on the hand-held radio, Douglas, smiled and said, "Have a good day, you two."

Jodie didn't answer. She just smiled.

Kalvin replied, "We will see you later."

As the taxi pulled up, they got into the back seat. Kalvin asked the driver to take them to Old Town, San Juan, to a bar restaurant he said he knew, Don Michelle's, about ten minutes from the dock.

Don Michelle's had a balcony with exotic plants. There were palm trees out in front by the steps. As Jodie stepped from the taxi she could see rattan tables and chairs with brightly covered cushions. The sound of Spanish music was drifting from the open doorway.

"It looks lovely, Kalvin."

She had to admit she was nervous.

"They do a good selection of light snacks, burgers and beers. They also play English TV."

Kalvin asked Jodie to find a seat and he went to the bar to get two beers. As he came back a man stopped to talk to him, he motioned with his left hand to indicate that he was with someone.

He sat down on the opposite side of the table to Jodie and passed her a beer. She looked lovely, her hair a soft brunette, her delicate skin bronzed from the sun, her make-up not overdone, just natural.

"Nice to get off and go ashore. Good job the weather's good today. I thought if it's OK with you we could walk into town and see the sights together?"

"Yes, it is nice to get away from the crowds. I love being at sea though, Kalvin, and everyone's so professional and friendly."

A short apprehensive silence fell between them.

"I'm a little nervous, Kalvin, being out alone with a guy. I've given up on boyfriends – they continually let you down, I'm not looking for a relationship, by the way," she said flatly.

Kalvin smiled. "Is that what made you come to sea – to get away from men and problems?"

"No, but yes as well. I've planned this since I was sixteen. I'm twenty-two, by the way."

He laughed, taking in what she said.

"I've just come out of a relationship myself – a young lady I got to know on an island. I found out she was seeing someone else."

Jodie was listening intently.

"That must have hurt and been a little bit of a let-down. I guess she was looking for something more permanent."

"I guess she was," said Kalvin.

"The guy I was seeing turned out to be a real rogue. He went off with my best friend and stole my car. I got the car back and haven't spoken to the so-called friend since! I am not good once I get mad. I do not back down! I never apologise," said Jodie.

"Sounds like she's the one that needs to apologise, Jodie."

"Thank you."

She started to look at him more closely: he had such deep-brown soft eyes and a laid-back manner to him, Jodie started to relax in his company.

"My dad died a few months ago and my mum lives on her own. I have three brothers and two sisters, who all said I should come, despite leaving Mum."

"Sound advice. That's a huge family, Jodie."

"Yes, they are all so great to me – all older. Of course, I miss my dad; he was such a kind man."

Kalvin just listened. Clearly this young lady, Jodie, had been through some tough times; she had her defences up and quite rightly so.

The waiter came over to take their meal order.

"Shall we head into town, then?" he asked.

"Yes, Kalvin, that would be great, I'm dying to have a guided tour."

"Ha ha! I'm not a tour guide, you know."

"Really?" she said sarcastically. "I thought you were."

They walked side by side along the crowded streets; Jodie could hear Spanish spoken by passers-by.

"We'll head to the church and historic buildings, then grab lunch at the restaurant called San Amigo's. They serve fish, burgers and chilli."

"Sounds fabulous, Kalvin. Wow! It's great to see and hear the local wildlife. I love the spring in England, it's really pretty here too."

"Your contract's for nine months?" asked Kalvin.

"Yes. And yours?" asked Jodie.

"Six months on and six weeks off all year. I signed up for ten years; it's been OK so far."

"How long have you to go until you finish?"

"Four years, I want enough money to buy a house outright with no mortgage; I live with my folks in Kent."

"OK – sounds a good plan."

Kalvin stopped as they neared a bar with outside tables. It looked busy.

"Here we are." He checked his watch. "Nearly 3 p.m. Are you hungry?"

"Yes, famished."

"OK! Let's get a seat."

They walked into the restaurant and sat over on the far side, where it was quieter. The waiter pulled out a chair for Jodie to sit down then left them to look at the menu.

"Have what you like, Jodie. I'm treating us."

"Thank you. That's nice of you, Kalvin."

Jodie studied the menu.

"I think I'll have a prawn cocktail, steak, salad and a glass of white wine."

"I'll have the 'surf and turf' with salad and a beer."

"This is a nice place, Kalvin." Jodie sipped her water, taking in the atmosphere in the bar. "I love the Spanish and Caribbean music mix."

"Yes, I like it here too. Paul and I come here to watch the English football games on TV."

"Which team do you support, Kalvin?" Jodie asked.

"Manchester City. They are not doing so well this year though – sold a few players off."

"My family support Southampton – avid season-ticket holders."

"OK. Do you like football, Jodie?"

"Not really. I love music, dancing, people and going places."

"Yes, I see that," he smiled.

Kalvin studied her, sitting back in the chair, relaxed. She had a great personality – so friendly, a little spoiled though. An innocent naivety shone out. He loved her deep-brown eyes and thick glossy hair. She had a style all of her own too, he noted. Smart, brave, intelligent and not afraid to say what she thought, but sensitive and caring.

"How's it been work-wise in the salon?"

"Yes, it's been interesting. Jayne's a little bit hard on us newbies. I am gradually getting used to the USA currency and getting used to being paid each month instead of each week. Passengers have so far been really nice – they love us English."

"Hmm. Jayne's not been well – she drinks a lot, I hear. So long as she's not bullying you?" he asked.

"No, it's OK; I just ignore her and go my own way."

"Good idea." He smiled.

Jodie loved the way he smiled from his eyes, she felt she could get to trust this man.

"The food on board the **Spring Sun** is a bit limited in choice. I like steak, but they cook it rare; I can't bear the blood running out. Breakfast is usually when I eat the most as I know what it is!"

Kalvin smiled and sat back to relax. "Yes, I agree with you there."

"Are you an officer, then, Kalvin?"

"Chief petty officer. More-senior officers get better privileges, like eating in the passenger dining areas. The ones at the darts match are OK guys."

"Yes, that was fun. Mike seems to think a lot of himself though, Kalvin."

"He's OK. He's got a lot of responsibility, he's been on board five months and will be going home on leave soon. OK – ready to order?"

The waiter came over directly as Kalvin motioned him with a 'come over' hand signal.

He wasn't drinking today, – three pints at the most. He wanted to give a good impression and, besides, he was responsible for getting Jodie back to the ship.

"One beer and a medium glass of white wine, please."

Ten minutes later, the food and drinks served, they tucked in. Silence fell between them as they ate. Jodie noticed Kalvin's mannerisms, he had good table manners, ate slowly and drank his beer really nicely.

Kalvin asked Jodie, "Whereabouts in Dorset do you live?"

"A town called Christchurch, it's about thirty minutes from Southampton. Do you know it?"

"No, but I have heard of it. I have family on the Isle of Wight. My sister and her husband live there."

"Oh, yes. Lymington's not far. The ferries go from there to Yarmouth."

"Seems far away when we are in the Caribbean. I do like the sunshine though. It will be cold in England now."

"Yes, coming into summer in a month's time."

"We are heading up the west coast of America in three weeks, after passing through the Panama Canal, Jodie."

"Yes, I am looking forward to that three-week cruise – different ports to explore. Will you get much time off, Kalvin?"

"Shouldn't be too bad – a lot of late shifts though. They change every six weeks. I am on either midnight till 4 a.m., 4 a.m. till 8 a.m., or noon to 8 p.m."

"Messes with your body clock, then?"

"Yes, sometimes. You get used to it though."

"My job's good with the hours. We even get a two-hour lunch break. I work from 9 a.m. till 1 p.m. and from 3 p.m. till 7 p.m. We only open in port for appointments. There's usually only one person on reception then, so we get lots of time to explore."

"Time to recover from a night out?" he enquired.

"Yes, and suntan time."

Kalvin finished his meal, sat back then waited for Jodie to finish hers.

"I'm a slow eater, Kalvin, the food is lovely."

"That's OK, Jodie – no rush. We're not due back on board until four thirty." He smiled then, looking at his watch. "It's only 3 p.m. – plenty of time. Another drink?"

Jodie smiled back, noticing how easy she felt in his company.

"Just a glass of water, thank you."

He called the waiter over to order one more beer for himself and water for Jodie. Jodie sat back after finishing her meal.

"That was delicious, Kalvin."

As they finished their drinks, there was a silence.

"We'll stroll back slowly, if that's OK?"

"Yes, that would be nice."

The waiter came over with the check. Kalvin took out his wallet and paid cash in American dollars.

"You ready, then, Jodie?"

"Yes, fine, head on."

She got up, put her purse on her shoulder, and then walked to the restaurant door followed by Kalvin.

They reached the dock where the **Spring Sun** was anchored, awaiting passengers with the gangway down. The officer with the radio was standing by. He saw Jodie and Kalvin approach the steps, instantly recognising them, letting the two on board.

At the top Kalvin turned to Jodie: "I have had such a great day, Jodie."

"Yes, me too, Kalvin. Thank you." She looked straight into his eyes and smiled.

Kalvin's heart melted, suddenly feeling so uplifted by the nearness of this enigmatic young lady.

"Can we meet up after we sail, Jodie?"

"I have to be in the salon until 7 p.m., Kalvin. I need to see Cherie also; she had a letter from home today."

"OK, I'll be in the crew bar. Come down when you are ready."

"Thank you for today again. Yes, I will see you later, Kalvin."

"OK, Jodie."

Jodie smiled again and walked to the left towards the stairs, forward of the ship.

Kalvin walked to the stairs to the right, the aft of the ship.

CHAPTER 5

"Goodbye, Cherie"

The passengers boarded and 'sail away' commenced. The horn sounded to announce their departure from the port of San Juan.

Jodie had changed into her uniform ready to go to work in the salon. She caught up with Cherie in the galley.

"Hi, Jodie. How was your day today with Kalvin?"

"Cherie, I had a great time, thanks. We went to a restaurant called San Amigo's for lunch and chatted for three hours."

"Wow! Jodie, that was nice."

"How about you?"

"I got a letter from home telling me my dad's poorly. Mum said she would call me if it got worse, the girls and I went shopping."

"Are you going into the salon? I'll wait for you to finish tea, I'm not hungry as I ate earlier."

"Yes, come and sit with me for a cup of tea?"

Cherie took her tray to the table, Jodie followed, then sat opposite her. Jayne came in to look for them.

"Hi, you two, I need you in the salon for five forty-five, after passenger drill."

"OK, Jayne, Cherie and I are just having a cup of tea."

"Don't be late."

"We won't!"

After she had gone, Cherie said to Jodie, "What is she like?"

They finished their tea, and then made their way with their life jackets to their assigned muster stations to show the passengers what to do in an emergency.

The officer on the bridge came on the Tannoy:

"This is a practice drill. All crew and passengers must attend. The ship's horn will sound seven short blasts and one long blast. Please have your life jackets with you. Crew will show you how you should wear these in an emergency. This drill is compulsory in regulations with maritime law. In case of an emergency all passengers and crew will now go to their assembly points to await further instructions.

"The next announcement will follow in five minutes."

The Captain announced:

"All persons have now been accounted for. Please stand down. Enjoy your cruise aboard MS *Spring Sun*.

"We will be setting a course for Barbados to arrive at 0700 hours tomorrow. Have a pleasant evening."

Once safety-at-sea drill was finished, Jodie took her life jacket back to her cabin; she went to knock on Cherie's door.

"Hi, Cherie. We may as well arrive in the salon together."

"OK, I'll just be a minute putting my lipstick on and changing my shoes."

"OK, Cherie," said Jodie. "Remember your name badge."

The girls made their way up to the salon.

As they walked in, Jayne pulled Cherie to one side: "Cherie, I've just had a call from the radio operator – they have asked you to go up to take a call to shore."

"Oh, is it from home?"

"Yes, Cherie." There was a degree of sympathy in Jayne's voice. "It is your parents."

"It must be my mum; my dad's been poorly."

Jayne turned to Jodie: "Man the salon, please, Jodie. Debbie will be here in a minute – she's gone to the Ladies."

Jodie tried to give Cherie a reassuring look, but she had this sinking feeling – her sixth sense – it was bad news. She hoped she was wrong.

"OK, Jayne."

"I'll come with you, Cherie," said Jayne. "Just for some support."

Clients started arriving for appointments. Jodie, Debbie and Tracy were kept busy until closing time at 7 p.m.

"Are you going to the crew bar, Jodie?" asked Debbie.

"I'll go if you are, I don't fancy getting dressed up. I wonder where the others are?"

"Let's go and find out how Cherie got on with the radio call," Debbie said to Jodie.

Debbie was from Liverpool, Jodie loved her warm and caring attitude and her party spirit.

"Yes, and later go to the disco, once the passengers have gone to bed, Jodie!"

"Great plan, Debbie!"

They both went down to the forward lower corridor, where their cabins were – four in a row. They were lucky to have one each.

Knocking on Cherie's door, there was no answer at first. They knocked again.

"Cherie, are you OK?" asked Jodie. "Can we come in?"

"No!" – followed by a whimper.

Then the door opened to a tear-stained face Cherie, her friend, usually so happy. Jodie went to her and held her.

"What's up, pet?" asked Debbie.

"It's my dad, Jodie," she managed to say in a trembling voice. "He died yesterday of a massive heart attack. My mum has asked me to go home, she's with my aunty. The funeral is Friday week."

Cherie burst into tears.

Jodie held her again, as if she was going to break like a china doll. Debbie got out the tissues, giving them to Cherie. They all sat on the bed.

"There, cocker, love, dry those eyes. It's dreadful news."

Like a mother hen Debbie took over and sat on the other side of Cherie to hold her hand.

Cherie wanted to talk: "He was getting over flu when I left, then he got worse and Mam said he had contracted pneumonia symptoms and was readmitted."

Both Jodie and Debbie looked at each other, as great minds think alike, they said together, "OK, Cherie, we'll help you pack."

"But first we'll get you something to eat," added Debbie. "It's nearly 9 p.m. I'm going to speak to the maître d' in the passenger-deck restaurant and get him to rustle something up for you." Debbie hugged Cherie. "Wait here, love, I won't be long, Jodie's here with you."

"Yes. Thanks, both of you," she managed in another wave of tears.

Debbie closed the cabin door quietly as she left.

"Cherie, do you have flight details yet?"

"Jayne's sorting it out. It's most likely to be St Martin on Friday. There's a flight from there to San Juan, then on to Miami and London. Mum's going to get Aunty Sarah to meet me and take me home to Cheshire."

"That sounds a good plan, Cherie." Jodie's sensible head was kicking in. "We have two days to have some fun before you leave. I know in your heart of hearts you won't necessarily feel like partying or going ashore, but, Cherie, we may never see each other again."

"Yes, Jodie, you're right."

"Remember when I first saw you at Heathrow Airport? I was a mess – so scared of flying – but determined! Well, it was down to you that I got here! You were amazing to me."

Cherie was about to cry again.

"Now dry those eyes, take a shower and we'll get you ready to have a few drinks and have some fun. You can't go anywhere at the moment – we are at sea."

"Cherie, it's your day off tomorrow, you and Debbie are free to go ashore till four. You can relax in the sun, then see Jayne about the paperwork."

"I'm going to miss you, Jodie."

"Cherie, I'm going to miss you too."

"Now let's find you something bright to wear." Jodie got up and started sorting through Cherie's wardrobe. "Pink number with black sequined jacket and stilettos?"

Cherie smiled, then got up to hug Jodie.

"I'll get showered."

Just then there was a knock at the door.

"Come in," they both said together.

"Room service," said Debbie.

Jodie opened the door and Debbie came in carrying a huge plate of triangular fancy sandwiches and cupcakes.

"Compliments of the maître d' – a swap for a shoulder massage. He says to give you his best wishes." She mimicked a strong Italian accent. "I'll put them over here, Cherie, on the dressing table. Oh yes! I also have champagne next door."

"OK, Jodie, I'll take that shower now or I'll miss out on the food. You two will have wolfed it back."

"Well, we may save you at least one, Cherie," joked Debbie.

"When you come out, Jodie will do your hair and I'll paint your toe and fingernails for you."

"And do your make-up. We'll also pour this champagne."

Cherie was smiling and crying all at once. She thought to herself, 'Leaving will be sad, but these memories of life on board will stay with me. Some of the best times!'

By the time they were all dressed and ready to go upstairs to the cocktail bar it was 10 p.m. The passengers were thinning out to go to the other bar, restaurants for extra food and after-show chats with the officers. This meant that they could enjoy themselves without being on show on their best behaviour. This evening was for Cherie and their friendship.

Jayne joined them, along with Lou Lou, who was a newbie. Jodie ordered four different cocktails: Rumba Banba, Sex on the Beach, Blue Island and Lagoon Sinful Sling. They were all decorated beautifully – Marc, the bartender, was an artist and took great pride in perfecting a beautiful drink.

"We are sorry to hear Cherie's sad news, and sorry to be losing her," he said to Jodie as he was making them up.

"Thank you – I'll pass that on to her."

"I'll bring these over on a tray. You go and sit down with the girls."

"Thank you, Marc."

"I want to make sure Cherie has something to remember her time on the *Spring Sun*, and the crew."

Jodie got off the bar stool and joined the girls at their table over by the window."

Marc was carrying the tray of cocktails over as Jodie relayed his message to Cherie that the whole crew were sad for her, and if there was anything they could do she only had to ask.

"There you go, ladies," he said as he placed each cocktail on the table with paper coasters.

Jodie went to pay.

He held his right hand up. "No charge – these are on me."

"Are you sure, Marc?" asked Jayne.

"Yes, with the bar's compliments."

"Well, come and join us in the crew bar tomorrow eve. We're going to party!" said Debbie.

"Great! I certainly will."

"Thank you, Marc," they said together. "Tomorrow's a

pink party, Marc – it's Cherie's favourite colour."

"OK, I'll hunt around for something – maybe ask the dressers for something from the show wardrobe."

"These cocktails are fab," Jodie said as she sipped hers with a straw.

"OK, a toast to Cherie! Cherie, we haven't known you for long, and your contract's being cut short, but you are like another sister to us. If everyone can raise their glasses, please . . ."

They clinked the glasses together, sipping their cocktails in unison, umbrellas near their noses. Laughter then, as Cherie's glacé cherry fell in her lap!

CHAPTER 6

Life at Sea and the Salon

Jodie soon became accustomed to the daily routines of working and living on board the **MS** *Spring Sun*, a lovely ship, beautifully decorated. The crew and officers were friendly and professional. Each person had a job to do; there was an understanding that even though there were different ranks, everyone had the interests of the passengers and ship uppermost in their thoughts each and every day. Life on board fell into a pattern. It was everything and more that Jodie had dreamed of.

She found getting around the ship very easy, and rarely used the lift. She went to the gym, swam and walked. Her figure was a slim size 12, her hair shone, skin was suntanned to a golden glow, which she had developed.

Treating each new day as an adventure, Jodie loved the work. The passengers, although challenging, were usually polite, friendly and they gave great tips. Jodie saved her money for trips ashore.

Her favourite island was Martinique, a French port where she and the girls would sit outside the cafés watching the rich and famous. They could also buy exclusive cosmetic brands at a fraction of the normal prices.

The cruises passed; then came the last week. They sailed from St Thomas to San Juan, where they stayed over before the next three-week cruise up to Alaska via the Panama Canal and the American west-coast ports. The itinerary changed for the summer – the summer would be spent cruising in Alaskan waters, with Vancouver as the home port.

Writing home regularly, Jodie received letters from

family every Saturday. When crew were going home they would take letters with them in their luggage to post for people as soon as they landed at Heathrow Airport. Each crew member was on a different-length contract. Jodie's mum said she once received two letters on the same day.

Jodie wasn't homesick at all, since Cherie's departure, she and Kalvin had been seeing each other on a regular basis. He was fun, genuinely a lovely person and someone she was becoming close to, although Jodie was aware he was going on leave very soon after the three-week cruise.

Salon life on the MS *Spring Sun* – the salon was set out to have two hairdressers, one hairdresser/barber and two beauty therapists. There was a reception area, a sauna and a shower. Situated on B deck, it was close to the swimming pool and sun deck. The stockroom was next to the salon with manager access only.

The passengers usually liked to come in to book in the mornings on the first day of the cruise to look their best for formal nights. The officers and crew came in for services before lunchtime on the quieter days.

Many famous guests came on board; one in particular, Jeanette Alexandria, from a British sitcom, was a graciously polite lady with very thick short hair. Jayne booked her in with herself.

Another part of the salon staff's duties was to dress the wigs for the dancers, for a French number they performed. Jodie and the girls also helped them backstage into their costumes. They weren't allowed to watch the shows, so this was a way to enjoy the music.

'Les Folies' – there were Angelique, Mitsy, Maisie and Josephine. The costumes were French fishnet stockings, bright-coloured corsets and plumes of feathers in the ringletted dressed wigs. Jodie loved to help. It was exciting to see the passengers' faces as the dancers went onstage.

The buzz of life on board. It was everything she had imagined it would be – her dream job, like no other way of life.

Every day was different – the travel to new ports, the people, the crew parties and the songs.

As the cruises rolled on, Jayne – the salon manageress – became a little more irrational, however. Jodie caught her drinking in the crew bar once, when she said she had to go and see an officer about a salon problem.

One afternoon, when the salon was quiet, Jodie decided she would speak to Jayne about her drinking problem. The girls had all said that they felt under more pressure because of Jayne's lack of professional conduct.

"Jayne," said Jodie, "are you well?"

"Jodie, my health is none of your concern," she replied sharply.

"Actually it is," persisted Jodie. "The girls and I have had a discussion with the ship's doctor, who is concerned as well."

"I have been getting back pains, stomach cramps and headaches. Alcohol eases it."

"The Doc can give you painkillers, you should go and talk to him about it."

"Yes, OK, I will."

"Well, you aren't any good to us as manageress if you aren't well."

"Yes, I'll go tomorrow."

"Right, Jayne, make sure you do."

"You're a good hairdresser, Jodie. I'm going to recommend to C-P Ltd they upgrade you to manageress on your next contract."

Jodie smiled at Jayne. "Well, that would be great, Jayne, but first things first: you have to get yourself sorted out. No drinking this evening – iced water or juice only."

"Bossyboots!" She smiled at Jodie.

Jodie smiled back, then gave Jayne a hug. "After work

I'm going to watch a movie with Kalvin. Fancy coming along?"

"No, thanks. I don't want to be a gooseberry."

"Ha! As if we would make you feel like that."

"Jodie, I am glad for you – he is a really genuine guy. You have only got to look, when he's with you, to tell he really cares."

"Yes, so do I – that's the scary part."

"You'll do OK with him, Jodie."

"I hope so, he is rather gorgeous."

Jodie said goodnight to Jayne, then went to meet Kalvin.

CHAPTER 7

Caribbean Romantic Adventures

Kalvin had arranged to meet Jodie in the crew bar at eight. Jodie just had time to go and change to meet him. He had said previously that he was on early shift. Jodie had the day off the next day in St Thomas.

Maurice was sat with Kalvin, he was as old as Jodie's dad would have been. He had been at sea on merchant ships since he was twenty-two. He was like Captain Bird, from the TV ad. An old hand with a new crew – Kalvin, Paul and Mick – the team of safety officers, who were very meticulous about their jobs. At the end of each day, they gravitated to the crew bar with an ice bucket of Budweiser's beers and some music from the old jukebox.

Jodie walked in and went to sit with them.

"Hi there, girl," said Maurice, holding his pipe to his lips. "Move over, lads. Let these lovebirds sit together!"

"Oh, Maurice!" said Jodie. "Do you need to embarrass me?"

Maurice chuckled, he liked this young lady too – loved to pull her leg. She reminded him of his daughter Louisa.

Jodie moved around the table to sit next to Kalvin.

"How was your day?" he asked.

"Yes, good. And yours?" She noticed he had a bandage on his wrist. "Did you hurt yourself, Kalvin?" She was concerned.

Maurice took a gulp of his beer and silence fell between the guys.

"It is nothing, Jodie. I caught it on a rope."

"Does it hurt?"

"Just aches a bit. I'll live."

"OK. Well, if it gets worse go see the Doc."

"Yes, I will. You ready to go to the movies?"

"Looking forward to it. Are you?"

"Yes, I'll just finish my beer and we will get going."

The jukebox was playing 'Everything Changes' by Paul Younger. The crew bar was as busy as usual. There were couples kissing in the corner on one side and some other deckhands talking and playing cards. Jodie sat patiently waiting.

Kalvin finished his drink. They both stood up together, said cheerio to the guys and walked through the galley to the corridor that led to the staircase to the main deck and forward to the cinema. The seas were a little rough that evening, the ship was rocking slightly. The crew were allowed to see movies on the big screen provided they did not take up passengers' seats.

Entering the dark room, they could see there were seats at the back on the far side. They made their way there together and sat down. The movie was just about to start, the title music of *Out of the African Jungle* sounded through the cinema. Kalvin sat with his good arm around Jodie as they snuggled up together.

Jodie felt safe in his company, she knew he wouldn't push his luck and rush her into an intimate relationship. She totally relaxed.

"You OK?" he asked her.

"Yes, thanks."

They sat through the movie, just happy to be close and enjoy each other's company. Eventually the lights came on again, the music playing. All too soon the film had ended.

"That was a lovely movie, Kalvin."

"Glad you enjoyed it, usually we get on-board movies that are ancient. That one's recent. They must be getting better at movie choices for the passengers." He looked at Jodie: "Fancy going out on deck?"

"Yes, that would be lovely."

They made their way on to the deck, the moon was up high in the dark starlit sky, its shadow reflecting on the rippling water as the ship cut through the sea. The Caribbean air was warm, breezy and balmy.

Kalvin took Jodie in his arms and kissed her tenderly. She kissed him back, her arms around his shoulders. They stood entwined for over twenty minutes, when they pulled apart every part of Jodie's body tingled.

"Jodie, I have so wanted to do that, I just wasn't sure you did as well."

She smiled. "Well, I wasn't sure either. You proved me wrong."

With his good hand he stroked Jodie's hair, then his hand glided to rest on her cheek. Jodie put her hand up to his.

"Now tell me how you really hurt your wrist."

"Not fooled easily, are you?" he said.

"No, I am not. One thing you will have to get used to is my female intuition."

"Hmm! Well, an officer said something I didn't like to hear. I took a swing at him and hit a door, sorry I lied."

She pulled him towards her. "Just don't do it again! Honesty's the best policy." Jodie spotted the time on her watch. "It's midnight, Kalvin. Tomorrow's a working day and you said you are on early shift."

"Yes."

"If you're the gentleman I think you are, you'll escort me to my cabin, sir!" She kissed him.

"With pleasure, madam."

He smiled, took Jodie's hand, then kissed her again. They walked arm in arm along the deck to the first doorway. Walking along the corridor, Kalvin turned to Jodie. There was no one else around.

"Jodie, would you like to see my cabin?"

"Mm." She thought for a moment. "OK, but just for ten minutes."

"That would be nice, I'll show you some pictures of home if you like."

"OK, lead the way."

They walked to the aft of the ship, then Kalvin opened a door which led to a narrow stairway. Jodie could hear the whirring of the ship's engines, then something else hit her – heat! It must be the laundry. Yes, she was sure that was what it was. Kalvin helped her down the stairway and past three closed doors. He got to the fourth and opened it with a key. Then he stood aside, for Jodie to enter.

"Here we are, Jodie," he whispered.

Jodie stepped inside, she guessed she must be below water level, as she couldn't see the water through the porthole, as it was closed and bolted. In her cabin the porthole acted as a window. The shower and toilet were in the same place as in her cabin. The bed was larger, the desk the same, and there was a larger wardrobe.

"Just popping to the bathroom. Take a seat, Jodie."

There wasn't anywhere else to sit but the bed, so she put her bag down on the desk and sat there.

The phone rang just then.

"Aren't you going to answer it, Kalvin?"

"No. It's the night watchman. I'm off duty – he just wants to chat."

Kalvin came in to sit next to Jodie.

"OK. Ah yes, photos."

He went to the bedside drawer and pulled out an album. Then put it on Jodie's lap. She opened it. Kalvin explained that the people in the pictures were his mum and dad, his sister Janice and her husband, Phillip. They were trying for a baby, but as yet with no luck. The pictures were taken on a holiday to the Isle of Wight.

The last page turned, Kalvin took the album and placed it on the desk.

She needed to excuse herself. Even though she really

liked him and trusted him, she wasn't in a hurry to get too close.

When she came back from the bathroom Kalvin was fast asleep on the bed with his clothes on.

Now she wasn't sure what to do – to stay or go? For a full five minutes she just stood watching him. He was out for the count.

Oh, hell, what a situation! She was too tired to make her way back to her cabin, and she wasn't sure of the way.

Jodie took off her shoes and hung her dress up on the door of the bathroom, she had her slip she could wear as a nightie. Then she lay down next to him, pulling the duvet over herself.

At three forty-five the phone rang, it didn't stop, Kalvin got up, said hi to Jodie.

"Have to go on watch," he said.

"Yes, Kalvin," she muttered.

"It's OK – you can stay. I'll be back at eight. I'll wake you and see you to your cabin."

"Thanks."

Putting her face in the palms of his hands, he bent over to kiss her, gently. Her skin was so soft.

"I had a lovely evening, Jodie," he said.

"Yes, me too, Kalvin."

He kissed her again gently.

"I'll see you soon. Sleep well."

Jodie settled down to sleep, despite the drone of the engines and the laundry. She dreamed of the moon, stars and warm sunny days.

Kalvin carefully closed the door so as not to startle Jodie. When he came back at 7.45 he opened it the same way. He put his cap on the desk, then went to the bathroom to wash and shave. The shift had gone OK. No disasters. They had docked in Barbados until 5 p.m. that afternoon.

He had enjoyed the evening with Jodie, he felt they got on very well. He was glad she felt able to trust him enough to stay. As he came out, refreshed, he went over, sat on the end of the bed and watched her. It was eight fifteen, she stirred.

"Hello, sleepyhead," he said, smiling down at Jodie.

"Hello, handsome!"

Kalvin moved closer, Jodie put her arms around his neck. A long, slow kiss followed.

"Mmm – nice way to wake up. I guess I had better get up. Are you going back to work?"

"Yes – we are in Barbados."

Jodie swung her legs to the floor, Kalvin passed her her dress.

"Can you show me the way back to my cabin?"

"Yes, Jodie."

She washed her face, combed her hair with her hands, then found her shoes and handbag.

"OK, let's go, then."

He opened the door to allow Jodie to go first.

"Walk to the end, Jodie, then take the stairs upwards."

Following Kalvin's instructions (he was right behind her), they popped out into a corridor amidships.

"I'll see you after work, Jodie. I'll pop by the salon."

They walked forward to the salon accommodation corridor.

"OK."

CHAPTER 8

The Boat Race, June 1985

It was a Monday, the ship was docked in Bridgetown, Barbados. They had docked one hour ago; Jodie and Kalvin were in the galley having breakfast before work.

Kalvin explained it was a long-standing tradition that went back centuries. When two ships of the same company were in the same port together, the crews would race in the lifeboats. It was a way of testing strength and promoting teamwork in the crews. In the olden days such races could also weed out the weaklings.

"Jodie, we are having a lifeboat race between the **MS Spring Sun** and the **MS Summer Sun** – the coxswains and the deck crew – this Friday in St Thomas. Should be fun to watch from the deck. It'll be a great race as long as the weather is good. It's a little colder now it's June," said Kalvin.

"Great! I'll round the girls up and we'll cheer them on!"

As usual, the salon girls were busy. These were the cheap-end cruises, they had been told. Passengers were given in their deal more on-board free spending money to spend in the bars, casino, shops and salon.

Kalvin and his team of safety officers were kept busy with maintenance of electrical safety, fire extinguishers, lifeboat equipment and all other things related to safety at sea. The week flew by, and then it was the port of St Thomas and the boat-race day.

Once the passengers had disembarked, the crew lowered the lifeboat into the water. The officers around the *Spring Sun* liaised with the *Summer Sun* officers for their crew to do the same. Both crews positioned the boats near the jetty, in line, with a rope in front of them to check they were level.

Standing in front of the jetty were the race captains, the first mates and the junior officers, on hand in case they were needed. There was tension as the rules were clearly read out by the **Spring Sun**'s first mate. Each craft had eight crew to row, one crew member to steer from the rear and one crew member to use the megaphone and shout instructions to the rest of the crew.

The Captain blew the whistle – one long sound to start the race. They were off!

The **Spring Sun** crew's rowing technique consisted of well-timed strong deliberate strokes. The **Summer Sun** crew's strokes were also strong, but slower.

Jodie and the salon girls, now with time to spare, were up on the passenger deck by the pool to watch this epic event. Having a good view of the whole race, a few of the bar stewards had joined them.

Darren, Larry and Howard started cheering and waving a banner!

"Come on, **Spring**! Come on, **Spring**!" They cheered. "You can do it!"

The girls joined in.

They were neck and neck at the halfway point, then the **Spring Sun** crew gave an almighty rowing stroke at a count of four, pushing them to the finish, bringing in the craft in a record time of forty-five minutes! The **Summer Sun** crew came in three seconds later – a close call!

The Captain blew the whistle twice – two short sounds to signify the end of the race – and announced the **Spring Sun** crew as the winners. A roar of cheers went up from the crew, the crowd watching, the salon girls and the stewards. They were the victors of the day winning the trophy for another time!

It was so exciting to watch; both captains shook hands and the crews rowed back to their ships, then prepared to winch the lifeboats on board and secure them in their places. Needless to say, all the crew from the **Summer Sun** lifeboat were invited on board the **Spring Sun** for lunch in the officers' mess and a few celebratory drinks.

CHAPTER 9

The Panama Run

At the end of June, it was time to leave the Caribbean behind, having collected passengers to do the three-week-long run through the Panama Canal and up the American west coast, cruising to the ports of Cartagena, San José, San Polenta, Acapulco, Los Angeles and San Francisco, heading towards Alaska. Their home port for the next four months would then be Vancouver.

Jodie was looking forward to it. She'd have lots of sea days, the tips would be great, and there'd be more time in the evenings to enjoy themselves. She would see the places that to Jodie, at school, had only existed on world maps.

She and Kalvin had grown closer, and, although their relationship wasn't intimate as yet, the closer she felt to him, the more she felt she would want to be intimate with him.

He was a genuinely dependable, easy-going person. When they were together they chatted about everything and shared many interests, especially music.

During the days that they were in port in the Caribbean, Kalvin's shift pattern fitted in with her own work schedule. They would go ashore as soon as they had docked, wander into the nearest town, explore, have a good lunch and a few drinks and just enjoy being a couple.

Kalvin was due to go home on leave at the end of the last cruise of the Alaska run, and, as if a built-in defence mechanism was there, the change of scenery had seen Jodie spending more of her evenings with the salon girls.

Kalvin, used to Jodie joining him at the end of the day in the crew bar, had missed her presence.

Kalvin came to see her at the salon, Jodie's manageress gave Jodie five minutes to talk to him, aware of their romance.

"Why are you avoiding me, Jodie?" he asked. "Have I upset you?"

"No, Kalvin, I'm just worried that we are getting too close. When you go home on leave I'm going to be lost."

"Tut! I will be back. It's not for long – only a few weeks." He sounded hurt and disappointed.

"Yes, I know, Kalvin. I'm just feeling unsure. I came to sea to see the world and work to save money."

"Yes, I understand, Jodie. Can we meet this eve on the crew deck and talk?"

"Yes, Kalvin – about 9 p.m.?"

"My shift's twelve till four, so yes, that's good. Jodie," he said, "I love you!"

Jodie smiled, surprised at his vocalised feelings for her. "See you this evening, Kalvin."

Jodie went back to her clients who were waiting for hairdos.

The Panama Canal – going through the locks. Jodie woke in her cabin on her day off, to see outside through the porthole a green bank. The ship had almost ground to a halt, which she presumed was due to the fact that the *Spring Sun* had reached the entrance to the Panama Canal and was in a queue.

She showered, dressing in casual light clothing, did her hair and make-up then made her way up to the crew deck. There were lots of restaurant staff and deckhands and some of the shop girls were watching the banks on opposite sides of the ship.

Being an observant person, Jodie asked a deckhand what he was looking for.

"Alligators. There are usually lots of them on the banks, today there are only a few," he said. "You have to look carefully as they aren't easy to spot. They camouflage well so that they blend in." He stood behind her, then pointed. "Yes, it looks green and scaly."

"Ah, I see," said Jodie. "Thank you."

He laughed, "Shy creatures with big teeth."

"Yes, I wouldn't want to get close to one."

"No," said Aran, "it would rip a human apart."

Jodie went up another deck and could see why the ship had slowed. Sure enough, a tanker longer than the **Spring Sun** was ahead of them. It was going to be a long day. It had also started to rain, so it was not a sunbathing day. She decided to go and get breakfast then sit in the library and maybe catch up on writing home to Mum and other family. Kalvin said he could take a letter for her and post it in London from the airport.

They had talked the night before last, and he had reassured her that he so wanted her and loved her. But he totally understood about her apprehension about being on a ship and having a relationship. It is an unreal environment and difficult with so many people around. He told Jodie again that he loved her, and she said that she thought the same; she just needed time.

Wanting to reassure Jodie, he said, "I may be going on leave, but my thoughts are with you. I'm looking forward to going home and doing ordinary things – seeing my parents and sister, watching Man City play on the tele – but I can assure you there is no one else and my thoughts are with you. Just you!"

They had kissed then, and Jodie stayed over with him in his cabin as they had before, wrapped in each other's arms until daybreak.

The next day was a day to gather her thoughts, and then that evening they had a crew party on deck to liven up the monotony of going through the Panama Canal locks. It would take, she had been told, three to four days, dependent on traffic.

The salon was open all day (eight forty-five until seven forty-five). She was thankful that their manageress had a rule that each staff member must have time out. A day off was a chance to explore, catch up on jobs like washing and ironing, meet new people and just be yourself. The weather was very humid, there was no air, so the library was the best option, air-conditioned and cool. Jodie found solace there.

The last big port before they reached the canal was Cartagena, the City of Emeralds, the crew called it – every jewellery person's paradise. There were also leather goods in the markets, she and Debbie had discussed a shopping trip and went in on the shuttle bus, with the passengers. Apparently if you took the bus you could be in danger from drug smugglers and muggers and, worse still, not come back in one piece!

The next day the **Spring Sun** was in place to go through lock 1. She went into the lock, which started filling up with water from the bottom and the ship floated slowly upwards, a bit like a toy boat in bathwater. It was odd to be floating, but not moving forward.

On day three – they were in the queue for the next lock. Ahead of the **Spring Sun** was the **Mystic Odyssey**; ahead of her was a tanker.

On day four – they were released into the lake, then the **Spring Sun** made her way to the next and final lock, to go down to sea level. Before long they were on their way again. The ocean was ahead of them along with many more exciting good times.

CHAPTER 10

Acapulco

It was the heat that hit Jodie as soon as she walked out on to the crew deck, it was so humid her lungs almost imploded as she struggled for breath. She found herself drinking water by the pint glass to quench her thirst.

The **MS *Spring Sun*** was docked overnight at Acapulco; the salon girls, including Jodie, decided that they would go into town as a group for a Mexican meal, meeting up with the shop and restaurant staff at a club named Punto's Palace for food, drinks and karaoke with Spanish-style entertainment. On the way in the taxi to the city, the girls sang Michaela Johnston's latest hit, 'You Start and Groove On', with the chorus of 'Groove on'. None of them knew the whole song, but all were in high spirits as they sang the chorus ten times, until they arrived at the venue.

Mexican music, a rich aroma of spices filled the air as the girls got out of the taxi and entered Punto's Palace. The rest of the group were already there waiting in the bar. Gary – the shop manager – went to speak to the restaurant manager about a table for sixteen, he asked for a view of the stage. They all settled into their seats and menus were passed around. The atmosphere was electric.

The group ordered cocktails: Wiki-ki, Singapore sling, Blue Lagoons, and gin and tonics, the party had started.

Then the host came onstage to welcome all the guests: "*Buenas noches* and good evening. Welcome to Punto's Palace – entertainment, Mexican food, local wines and excellent Mexican hospitality! Eat, drink, enjoy."

"We welcome our first act, Julio Malino, a local Mexican/Spanish guitarist with an amazing sexy voice – one for the ladies!"

Julio came onstage and stood to the left of the host. He took a bow.

"Julio," he gestured, "the stage is all yours."

Julio sat down on a stool and adjusted the microphone to his height.

"Good evening, everyone." He spoke into the microphone and strummed his guitar. "Now I wonder who will come onstage and sing a song with me?"

A silence fell in the room, he spotted Jodie.

"How about the lady in the red dress?"

The crew started clapping and cheering for Jodie to go up and join Julio.

"Go for it, Jodie," said Debbie.

She smiled, got up from her seat and made her way to the stage amidst whistles, cheers and clapping. He held out his hand to help her up the steps. Jodie went to stand next to him. Taking the microphone off the stand, he put it to Jodie's lips.

"Hello, Julio," she said.

"Hello" – swapping the microphone to his mouth. "What's your name?"

"Jodie Hayes." Jodie looked him straight in the eye.

More wolf whistles from the crew.

"You have quite a following there, Jodie!"

"Yes, we are the crew from the **MS Spring Sun**, in port overnight. We all work very hard; I am a hairdresser the bar staff, restaurant staff and main deck crew are here. Getting ashore is a great change."

More whoops and cheers.

Julio, laughing: "You may just outshine me tonight Jodie."

"Well, Julio, let's see who's the best singer, then!" she said into the microphone.

"I must say, Jodie, you look lovely this evening."

"I bet you say that to all the girls, Julio."

"Ha ha! Are you nervous?"

"Of you? No! I'm used to public speaking and I sing when I'm happy."

"What are you going to sing this evening, Jodie?"

"On the way over I decided I would sing two songs. The first is 'A Powerful Love' by George Windfall. And he second is 'I Am What I Am' by Cathy Moosetti."

"Great choices, Jodie."

Jodie stood behind the microphone. "Hi, all. Please eel free to join in the choruses."

She started her song interpretations, and then held he microphone out to the audience to join in, telling hem in the chorus they weren't loud enough.

The room exploded into a louder than usual full :horus of 'A Powerful Love', followed by more cheers ind whistles.

"Thank you, everyone. Julio, would you like to join in vith guitar in the next song?"

Julio came back onstage. He spoke into the nicrophone and hand-motioned to Jodie. "Jodie, a ¡reat performance. I'm not sure, you may put me out ιf a job!"

"Ah, but you have such a lovely way to strum those :hords!"

More cheers and laughter from the audience.

"You see, Julio, it is what delights the audience."

"We had best get started, then," he replied as he trummed a chord on the guitar.

They sang a duet of 'The Lady in the Red Dress', aking it in turns with the verse, and the audience took ɔ the floor to smooch-dance.

At the end Julio bent forward to kiss Jodie's cheek.

She spoke to him without the microphone: "Thank you. 's been fun."

He took her hand. "You are very beautiful, Jodie."

Smiling, Jodie said a gracious goodbye then, amongst more clapping, rejoined her group.

More than six songs from Julio later, the evening came to an end; they ordered a taxi then went back on board the **MS *Spring Sun***.

Jodie made her way to the crew bar, where she found Kalvin waiting up for her.

"Hey there," he said as Jodie sat with him. "Did you have a great time?"

"Yes, fabulous."

As Jodie relayed the evening to Kalvin, he felt a bit jealous, he wished he could have been there.

"He was a real smoothie though, Kalvin."

"Sounds as though it's a good thing you are spoken for!"

"Hmm, yes, it is!"

"I'll finish this pint and we'll go out on deck to look at the city lights. It's a lot cooler now, I'm on duty at four to get ready for 'sail away' at 5 a.m."

"OK, great!" She smiled up at Kalvin and gave him a cheeky kiss on the forehead.

CHAPTER 11

Los Angeles: The City of the Famous

After the three-week cruise through the Panama Canal, there was an air of excitement and anticipation amongst the crew of the **MS *Spring Sun***. Officers, hotel staff and staff from all the shops and the salon were looking forward to a coach trip to Disneyland and Universal Studios.

Rumours of the famous people they might meet, the characters from the movies, real quarter-pounder beefburgers and Coke bottles were a real attraction. As the ship sailed into Los Angeles, the horn was sounded amidst the ships already berthed. Extra flags had been added to the ship to set the tone. Once the usual checks had been made, breakfast finished and the passengers disembarked, the group met on the crew gangway to take the coach on the highway.

There were eighty crew members, spread over two coaches. Jodie and Kalvin sat together a row behind the front seats. Debbie and Julie were behind, followed by Bungie and Trevor with the shop girls.

As soon as the coach had pulled away from the dock on to the freeway, the songs started, including 'We're All Going on a Summer Holiday' by Clifford Rushard and Paul Younger's 'Everything Changes'.

On the third song, 'You'll Never Get to Heaven in a Baked-Bean Tin', they were almost at the Disney Park, Los Angeles. The coach pulled in and the driver reminded the passengers to be back on board by 6 p.m. The *Spring Sun* was on an overnight stop; however, some crew members had to be back on duty.

Jodie and Kalvin were amongst the lucky ones who didn't need to work for the whole day, so they planned a quiet dinner, which Kalvin had arranged in the passenger restaurant. Kalvin had a surprise for Jodie.

On entering the Disney wonderland, the group set a meeting point and went in different directions. Jodie and Kalvin went towards the Magic Kingdom, where they saw signs to the water rides.

"Jodie, are you up for getting a bit wet?"

"Yes, Kalvin, so long as we can get a drink afterwards. It's a lovely warm day."

"Great!" he said, holding Jodie's hand and leading her to join the queue.

The sign said, 'Queuing Time 20 Minutes'. It was held up by Tigger, who came over and put his hand on Jodie's shoulder.

Kalvin got out his camera and took a picture of Jodie and Tigger.

"Smile! One for the album!"

Mickey Mouse joined them.

"Can I have a picture of you and me with Tigger?"

Kalvin gave his camera to Mickey, who snapped two shots of Jodie, Kalvin and Tigger, whose tail came up around them both.

Five minutes later, they were at the front of the queue. People were laughing, shouting and screaming as they were enjoying the Magic Kingdom ride.

Jodie and Kalvin got on, strapped themselves in and waited to move forward. As the ride started Jodie was a little nervous. Kalvin held her hand, sensing her nervousness.

The ride rolled along, turning to the side through fake caves with water jets coming in from the sides, then they were taken out into the open from a height and finished back where they started.

Yes, they were wet.

"How was it for you, Jodie?" Kalvin asked.

"Yes, fun," she replied. "I'm wet through!"

"Let's get a drink and sit out by the aquarium."

"Great idea!"

The aquarium was amazing. As they walked through the tunnel, sharks swam back and forth. Turtles in the large tanks were swimming gracefully then floating in the water. Some dolphins swam to the side of the tank, making noises. Then they swam off to the middle, jumping up and splashing. It was all so magical. Jodie felt as though she were in a dream. It *was* a dream – being out for the day with Kalvin and the crew at Disneyland – a dream she did not want to wake up from.

All too soon it was four thirty and time to head back on the coach to the *Spring Sun*, to life on board. Once everyone was ready to go, the coach started up, leaving the park. All the people, tired from the day, were quiet and sleepy. Jodie nestled into Kalvin's shoulder and slept all the way back. The coach ground to a halt to the right of the dock where the **MS** *Spring Sun* was tied up for the night in Los Angeles waters. Kalvin kissed Jodie on the forehead.

"OK, sleepyhead, time to wake up," he said, smiling down at her.

"Back already?" she asked.

"Yes, we are," he said.

Jodie reached up and kissed him. "I've had the best day ever."

He kissed her back. "So have I," he said, "but we are not quite finished yet. Tonight I've arranged for you and I to have dinner in the passenger restaurant around seven thirty."

"That sounds fab, Kalvin."

"I hope you like it. It's the basic menu, but chef said he would have a word with the maître d' to put on a bottle of wine."

Jodie thought, 'How did you manage that?' There were strict rules about crew dining in the passenger restaurant.

"I arranged for him to have his shower fixed with maintenance ahead of schedule."

"Ah! Clever move."

"He was chuffed when I told him I'd fitted a new shower head as well; it's been dodgy since three cruises back."

"OK, shall we meet up in the crew bar? I'll need a shower and a change of clothes. I'll need to wear a posh frock to dine in the restaurant."

"Yes, fine," said Kalvin. "Time to get off this coach, we are the last ones on here."

"Oh!" giggled Jodie. "I hadn't noticed."

She got up, as she was in the aisle seat, followed by Kalvin; they grabbed their bags, thanked the driver and walked hand in hand to the ship's gangway.

Jodie got back to her cabin, showered then looked for something to wear. After a lot of thought, she decided to go for her long red dress and a shrug, with her black patent stilettos. Her jewellery included simple crystal earrings with a chain.

When she was ready, she checked the time: six twenty. Kalvin would be in the crew bar. She looked at her reflection in the dressing-table mirror. Her bronze tan had faded a little now they were heading along the west coast of America, but she still felt it made her look healthy. Her hair was a light blonde, her make-up not too dramatic. Yes, she would do!

Making her way to the aft of the ship, she saw two other officers, Charles and Gerald. They did a double take at Jodie; she ignored them and walked on.

Jodie reached the crew bar, looking for Kalvin. She was looking for a guy in faded blue jeans and a white T-shirt. No one there fitted that description; there was only Douglas and a guy in a blue navy suit. Not sure what to do, she went to the galley to look for him there.

Kalvin spotted her as she walked out of the bar, he was the guy in the suit. He caught up with her.

"Jodie?" He reached for her hand.

She turned around.

"Kalvin?"

He grinned. "Yes, one and the same."

"Wow! You look so handsome and smart. I'm sorry I didn't recognise you!"

"Well, I would hardly turn up in jeans! I thought when you went out of the crew bar you had changed your mind. You look amazing, by the way." He offered her his arm. "I believe the passenger restaurant is this way, one deck up."

Jodie linked her arm in his, as they made their way to the restaurant for a romantic meal for two. Kalvin stood back for Jodie to enter first. The waiter led the way to the back, to a table with a sea view. He pulled the chair out for Jodie to sit down, Kalvin sat opposite.

"This is lovely, Kalvin."

Kalvin was really pleased Jodie liked the table. She looked stunningly beautiful in that long red dress, he couldn't take his eyes off her.

"Shall we look at the menu?" Jodie picked it up. "There's so much, Kalvin. Is it free?"

"No, but it is discounted just for us."

"I'll have to give whoever it is a half-price haircut."

"Yes, he would like that."

Just then the waiter came over.

"I'm Milo. I will be looking after your wine and meal service this evening. What will it be for madam?" he asked Jodie.

"I would like a Chardonnay – large glass."

"OK, I'll go with the same," said Kalvin.

"Sir, may I recommend the Californian Chardonnay?"

"I'll take your word on that. Could we have the ice bucket, please?"

"Yes, of course."

Milo left the two to enjoy their wine while they thought about their menu choices, he came back over after ten minutes.

"Madam, what would you like to eat – fish, chicken or beef?"

"I'll go for chicken chasseur, please." Jodie handed Milo the menu.

"I'll have beef Wellington, Milo. Thank you," said Kalvin.

"Kalvin, I can't believe my life at the moment, it's like a perfect dream."

"You're perfect, Jodie. You're fun to be with, kind, loving, even-tempered except when you're tired . . . and I love you so much." He looked directly into Jodie's eyes as he said it.

"Kalvin, that's lovely. No one's ever said those things to me before."

The main course arrived within twenty minutes, they ate slowly.

"Kalvin, this is great – eating here, just like the passengers."

"Yes, it is – makes a change."

The waiter, Milo, came back to check on them.

"Is everything OK for you both?"

"Yes, thank you – very nice, Milo."

"Coffee and amaretto liqueurs are nice after a meal. Shall I order these for you?"

"Yes, that would be lovely. About fifteen minutes, Milo? Give us some time."

"With cream or without?"

"With cream, please, Milo."

"I'll have the same, Milo, please."

He went away; they finished their meal.

Kalvin couldn't wait any longer: "I've a present for you, Jodie."

Out of his jacket pocket he took a long blue velvet box and placed it in the middle of the table opened. Inside was a gold engraved bracelet. It said, 'Jodie'.

"Kalvin, it's beautiful."

"It's engraved on the back, take a look."

Jodie took the bracelet out of the box and turned it over. It said, 'S.W.A.L.K. 06-06-1985'.

"Thank you, Kalvin."

"Shall I put it on for you?"

Just then Milo came over with the coffees, he set them down.

"Kalvin, it is lovely. Yes, please."

Jodie put her left wrist on the table and Kalvin put the bracelet on for her, closing the clasp. She held it up to admire it, a broad smile came over Kalvin's face.

"It looks great on you, Jodie, and I think I've achieved the impossible: you're lost for words!"

"Ha ha! Yes, I am." She looked at those deep-brown eyes and tanned skin. "Better drink this coffee, Kalvin."

"Yes," he said, still smiling.

"I'm never taking this off. Thank you Kalvin."

He was silent for a moment.

"A special gift for a special lady."

"It's been a special day, Kalvin."

"Yes, it has. Shall we go outside, Jodie, after our coffees?"

"Yes, that would be lovely."

Milo came over to collect the coffee cups. Kalvin tipped him $10.

"Thank you, Milo," said Jodie. "It was a lovely meal – great service."

"You're welcome."

Jodie walked to the end of the restaurant, then out on to the passenger deck. It seemed odd to be on board with no motion as they were tied up in port overnight with just the sound of the breeze in the air. The city's lights were bright, like glittering stars, twinkling over the city of Los Angeles.

Kalvin put his arms around Jodie's waist, stood behind her and held her tight. It was at that moment Jodie knew they would be forever friends. They stood taking in the night, overlooking the famous city of Los Angeles, California, USA.

CHAPTER 12

I Left My Heart in San Francisco

The salon was as busy as ever, with people coming and going. The girls in the salon Jodie had got to know were now a solid team, the routine of each new cruise becoming a familiar part of everyday life. After leaving Los Angeles, the next exciting port on the west coast of America was San Francisco.

Jodie was up at five to be on deck and be ready to sail under the Golden Gate Bridge at dawn. It was an overnight stay, and again Kalvin and Jodie could go ashore. They had been talking about having a meal in the Fisherman's Wharf area, then going to a hotel to spend the night together.

As the **MS *Spring Sun*** got closer to the Golden Gate Bridge, the passengers were flocking on deck and cameras were clicking. Jodie and the salon girls were enthralled. The feeling of seeing such an engineering feat of achievement was awesome – the sheer size of the bridge! Its colour was like that of no other bridge Jodie had ever seen. It was simply magnificent. Jodie asked a crew member to take her picture on her disc camera with the bridge in the background.

She went to work that morning before they docked, for passengers to make appointments for the next day. Then came the anticipation of a very special night ahead.

Kalvin had booked a hotel with a view. Jodie had no idea where it was in the city. He had rung, he said, from San Diego to check they had a vacant double room with a bath. As there were only showers on board, the thought of a soak in a large tub with bubbles was a luxury that excited Jodie, and the intimacy of sharing that luxury with a person she loved was even more enticing. She had made a special effort to look her best in a silky red dress and low heels for walking.

They met as usual on the gangway, said hello, showed their crew passes to the officer on watch and made their way along the Fisherman's Wharf to the restaurants, on the jetty.

The lights from the city were bright; people were laughing, drinking and enjoying their time together. Jodie took Kalvin's arm. She felt so safe with him beside her. They strolled along as if they had known each other for years, enjoying the moment, soaking up the sights, scents and atmosphere, feeling free of the constraints of ship rules.

They stepped into the hotel lobby of Esporato Magnificent, which was huge; a large chandelier hung from the ceiling and artworks adorned the walls with a circular desk in the middle of it. Classic elegance in every corner the eye could see! Jodie was speechless. Kalvin made his way to the desk and announced their arrival. He watched Jodie's face and smiled to himself.

"Hello. I've booked a room – Kalvin Wheeler and Jodie Hayes – overlooking the bay."

The receptionist looked in the reservations book.

"Yes, Mr Wheeler. Do you have luggage?"

"Just two overnight bags. We have to be on board by eight tomorrow morning, we are crew sailing on the **MS Spring Sun**."

"Yes, Mr Wheeler, that's fine. Would you like an early morning call?"

"Yes, that would be good."

The receptionist handed Kalvin a key to the allocated room and gave him directions: "Take the lift to the tenth floor, turn right and your room is 1008. If there is anything you need please call down by telephone."

"Thank you. Could you send up a bottle of champagne and a round of sandwiches – ham and cheese – and crisps?"

"Yes, certainly."

"Thank you," said Kalvin as he picked up their bags.

Jodie followed him to the lift, they entered and made their way to the hotel room, which seemed to Jodie a very long way up.

They got out, then walked along the corridor. Kalvin held the door open for Jodie to enter first, then followed her in with their overnight bags, closing the door carefully behind him.

Jodie went to open the curtains, as she did so, she saw the **Spring Sun** below, across the harbour from the hotel. Lit up in front of them, in all her glory, was the ship that had become home.

"Wow," she said, "isn't she incredibly beautiful at night?"

Kalvin put the luggage on the rack and came over to Jodie. He put his arms around her, holding her to him, then kissed her gently on the neck.

"Yes, you are," he said to Jodie.

"It is a great view from here."

Jodie turned to Kalvin, she kissed him passionately.

"Mmm," she said, "you're such a romantic, Mr Wheeler."

"I try my best," he said.

Just then room service arrived with the champagne. Kalvin tipped the waiter. He left, Kalvin poured champagne into the crystal wine flutes.

"Let's sit on the floor, Kalvin, and enjoy the view of the lights over the harbour of San Fran."

Kalvin took the cushions and pillows off the king-size bed and put them on the floor to be more comfortable.

Sitting down, Jodie said, "What shall we toast to?"

"To lots of good times together, Jodie."

"Yes, and love," she said.

Two glasses each – they finished the champagne and ate the sandwiches. Then Kalvin ran the bath, filling it with bubbles. Giggling by then, Jodie felt like a teenager on her first date.

"I think you may be a bit tipsy, Jodie."

"Kalvin, want to help me undress?"

"I would love to," he said.

He took the glass from her hand then gave her a long, slow kiss. He undid the zip on her dress, which slid to the floor, leaving Jodie in her underwear. Then he undid her bra, carefully slipping his hand around Jodie's waist, and removing it from her breasts. He kissed her neck, her shoulders, holding her to him. Jodie loved his touch.

"Want to step into the bathroom, Jodie? Share a bath with me?"

"Wonderful, lead the way."

Kalvin took Jodie's hand and led her to the perfumed bubble bath. Scents of lavender, white tea and roses filled the air.

She removed her underwear and stepped in, feeling the warmth of the water surround her naked body.

Kalvin undressed, and got in.

"Mm," said Jodie, "I've missed having a bath. Showers don't give you this lovely feeling as if you're floating."

"Yes – such a lovely feeling," said Kalvin. "American baths are large – big enough for two."

They stayed in until the water got cold, Kalvin got out first, then held out his hand to help Jodie. Towel in hand, he rubbed her dry, then wrapped her in a bathrobe and she did the same for him.

He dried her feet once she was sat in the chair. A long, slow kiss followed, then Kalvin led her to the bed. Holding her, he took the robe from her shoulders, parting it slowly, he then kissed every part of her body. Jodie was tingling all over, her breath deep, her feelings for Kalvin overflowing with such longing.

Kalvin looked at her naked body. "You are so beautiful, Jodie. I love you so much."

She sensed his nearness, his body's desire growing. She pulled him to her, removed his gown and their passion for each other became one.

CHAPTER 13

Vancouver, BC: The Dry-Dock Holiday

As the **MS *Spring Sun*** made her way into Vancouver Harbour Jodie felt an air of anticipation for in the middle of this month they would be in dry dock. The ship was due to go in for a refit and repairs, allowing time for a vacation. The girls got together one evening after work for a sauna and decided to book a stay in a hotel on Vancouver Island with a spa.

"It will be so nice to have a bath," said Jayne.

"Yes, a real soak with lots of bubbles, and be still. Although I like the movement of the ship I do miss not moving, waking up and seeing trees and hearing the birds."

"Being at sea is great, but I do miss being able to walk down the street or drive a car to a supermarket."

"Nine months isn't that long though, we are four months in, you and I."

"For Allanah it is seven, she's getting tired."

"Yes, she's gone to bed early this eve. She said to fill her in at breakfast when we've decided where to go."

"Well, I've found out through the port rep that there's a great hotel called Galliano. It's on the north side of Vancouver Island, it has bars and restaurants nearby."

"That sounds great. Can we book it through her?" asked Mich.

"Yes, she said it's just a phone call next time we're in port."

"There's three more cruises before we go into dry dock – three more commission slips – so if we pull together, the six of us, we should be OK for money."

"Yes, Tracy. We'll give Arriana a deposit and ask for a receipt for the cash."

"Good plan, Jodie."

"It's just a taxi ride," said Jayne.

"Kalvin knows the taxi firm, I'll ask him to help get a price for us there and back. Pre-bookings will probably be cheaper."

"OK – can't wait. I'm going to work extra-hard to get tips, I don't want to use my savings."

"I love using this sauna, but it is so hot."

"Yes, time to get out, Jodie."

"Me too," said Mich.

"Me too," said Jayne.

The girls got dressed then headed to bed. Tomorrow night was a formal night, and they needed to be on their toes with the passengers, who, according to the shop girls, were pretty demanding.

Next day they were in Juneau, the capital of Alaska. It consisted of three bars, a hotel, a bank and a food store. The hotel, however, did have a dance floor upstairs, and it happened that on the Monday when the *Spring Sun* was in port they had a disco.

It was a long stay – 'sail away' wasn't till two in the morning, allowing for people to make the most of an evening ashore, which the bar staff did as it was quiet on board. Bars were open, but there was minimal staff.

Kalvin, Paul, John, Mich, Jayne and Jodie wandered into town to the hotel disco about 8 p.m., it was empty. It had been raining, so a lot of the passengers had stayed on board. The DJ was playing 'Born in the USA' by Barry Steen. The girls got up to dance and the guys stayed at the bar.

Exhausted, it wound down by ten thirty. Kalvin and Jodie were the last to leave to make their way back. The rain had become heavier. They both got soaked to the skin, with dripping-wet hair.

Douglas was on the gangway.

"You two look like drowned rats, you'd best get out of sight before people see you."

"Thanks, Douglas," said Jodie.

Kalvin and Jodie made their way to the aft of the *Spring Sun* and Kalvin's cabin, he opened the door to let Jodie in first.

"We'd best get in the shower," he said as he saw Jodie shivering.

He turned it on, they took off their wet clothing and got in. Kalvin's arms around Jodie felt to her like such a safe place to be. She could feel the warmth of his body against hers, his kisses so tender and his genuine love.

He took the soap and washed her back and shoulders, then her breasts and thighs. Jodie held his shoulders so as not to slip. Luckily the *Spring Sun* was still in port. If she'd been moving it would have been tricky to keep their balance. Jodie rinsed off.

"Thank you. I'll get out and let you have space."

Jodie stepped out carefully and wrapped herself in a bath sheet, drying her hair with a smaller towel, she sat on the bunk; Kalvin came and joined her. He kissed her, holding her close.

"You smell so good, Jodie."

"Well, you do too," she giggled.

"Best get to bed, we've both got to be up in the morning early."

"You're on watch duty at four?"

"Yes."

"I'll just brush my teeth, Kalvin, and put on a nightie."

"OK."

Kalvin got into bed, Jodie then cuddled up to him. The warmth of his nearness floated over her body, sending her into a deep relaxed sleep.

Dry dock

The girls packed up the salon, put away the stock in the cupboards, locked away the electrical equipment and cleared away everything else that could possibly be of use to non-professional people.

The taxi to take them all to the Hotel Galliano on Vancouver Island was arriving at one. All the girls had packed their luggage the night before and were ready to go. They all had a cooked breakfast, so only needed dinner at the hotel. All were very excited.

The *Spring Sun* was to be three days in dry dock. The conditions weren't good. The galley was on a two-hour window to save the generators that were in place. It was hot on board. Workmen would be everywhere, with the lifts not in use, water usage limited and carpets up in all the lounges and restaurants. Chaotic! There was little or no air conditioning.

They all met by the gangway, suitcases in hand ready for the waiting taxi. One by one the girls walked down the gangway, waiting for each other at the bottom.

"Jayne," said Jodie, "did you pack a hairdryer?"

"Yes, but they should have one there."

"Good point."

"Allanah, have you brought the champagne for later?"

"Yes, Jodie, and the largest box of chocolates I could get my hands on!"

"Great!"

"Hi there, ladies," said the minibus driver in his Canadian accent.

"Hi there," they said to him together.

"You gals all together?"

"Yes."

"Your fare's already paid for."

"Really? Who by?"

"He said his name was Kalvin Wheeler."

"Oh," said Jodie. "He didn't say to me he'd paid for it!"

Jayne said, "He's such a generous guy, Jodie. You are lucky."

"Yes, he is. I'll thank him when I get back."

"Make sure you do, Jodie. He's worth holding on to," said Allanah.

Once they were all in, the driver took them to the water bus that went to the island. It would take an hour to cross. The weather was warm and slightly breezy. Jodie and Jayne went to the front of the ferry. They saw the island in the distance.

The boat was full – children, grandparents, some wheelchairs and dogs. It was hard to get a seat, so the girls stood most of the way. They picked a spot on the starboard side, from where they could see Stanley Park, with the *Spring Sun* to the right of it.

Three days and nights with no work – just eating, sleeping and relaxing. It was going to be amazing!

The water bus came into the port on Vancouver Island. In clear view were the red London buses that had been shipped over and made into restaurants – a tourist attraction – Canada being part of the British Commonwealth.

Once they were all together, the girls found a taxi to take them to the Hotel Galliano. It was a fifteen-minute ride. They passed large houses with large cars parked in the driveways, blocks of condominiums and slick-looking shops with restaurants above them.

They arrived at the hotel in the late afternoon. Jodie tipped the driver and they all made their way into the lobby. Guests were relaxing in the conservatory area, which looked over a small lake.

Jayne took charge: "Hello. We have a reservation for three rooms, booked in the name of the beauty girls of the *Spring Sun*. We are taking a few days' rest while our home's in dry dock."

The receptionist looked at her book. "Yes, ma'am, I can see." She went to the key rack and took out three room keys. "You're on the fourth floor – the three rooms are next to each other. The health suite is included in your price. All details of opening times and treatments are in the brochures in the rooms. The lift is to your left of reception. If you wish to book dinner please call down before 6 p.m."

"Thank you." Jayne took all three keys and passed two to the other girls. "Right, let's go, girls."

They made their way to the lift, pressed the button and alighted on the fourth floor. As they entered the rooms the girls instantly felt at ease.

"This is amazing. Jayne, you're a marvel," said Jodie.

"Bags the bed on the right."

"OK. They are queen-size – we can spread out! No single bunks."

Jayne put her case on the bed then went to check out the bathroom.

"Jodie, there's a corner bath."

"Wow, fab! Let's run it now and get the bubbles going. You can go first, Jayne, as you did all the hard work of booking everything."

"Thanks, Jodie."

"I'm real tired. I need a snooze, then I'll go in and you can order dinner for seven thirty. Check with the others first though."

Jodie lay on the large bed and she could hear oohs and aahs as Jayne got into the Jacuzzi corner bath with the lavender bubbles. She smiled to herself as she had her snooze. This was great. Working solid from nine until seven, six days a week, and going out every evening on the ship had been a constant routine. This was a lovely rest.

The girls were looking glamorous when they closed the door of the hotel room to meet the others.

"I'm famished," said Allanah.

"Me too," said Jayne.

"I could down a cocktail or two."

"That bath was to die for!"

"You enjoyed it, then," said Jodie.

"Did you notice?"

"Yes," she giggled.

Then they linked arms.

Dinner was a selection of chicken, beef and fish with salad, garlic bread and a side order of olives.

The hotel manager took a shine to Allanah, who being blonde, slim and six feet tall turned heads wherever she went.

He said to Allanah, "Would you like to choose the wine from the menu, beautiful lady?"

He passed her the menu and she studied it closely.

"We will have the Chardonnay – your largest bottle – six glasses and an ice bucket, please."

She turned her head and gave him her widest smile, staring straight at him, looking cool and innocent. He was clearly blushing.

Jodie smiled, trying not to laugh. Allanah could be so mischievous when she wanted to be. After he had gone, they all looked at each other and tutted at Allanah.

"You're a vixen."

"What?" she said.

"Tut-tut!" said Jayne.

"Well, we want good service, don't we?"

"Yes, we do."

The wine arrived and the glasses were filled. Jodie raised hers in a toast.

"To us and friendship," said Jayne.

Together they all said, "Here's to life at sea!"

Chink, chink!

Back on board the *Spring Sun*, the guys were working from nine to five. Kalvin liked this – it was better than the unsociable shift pattern they usually had to do. They finished, went into Vancouver, found a bar, played pool and chilled, cracking jokes there and back. They were a bit worse for wear from a few drinks.

On the third night Kalvin said to Paul, "I think I'd rather go to bed early tonight – can't do with another headache."

"Really?" said Paul. "We just got going. Next week you'll wish you could go out."

"Jodie's back tomorrow. I want to be sober. It's OK for you, you don't have a girlfriend."

"Is it serious between you two?" asked Paul.

"She's an amazing person. Yes, I think it could be. I'm thinking about settling down in five years' time."

"Five years is a long time, Kalvin. How do you know she doesn't want to carry on travelling? It's what she signed up for."

"It's only nine months."

"Most of the hairdressers do at least two to three contracts. It's a cheap way to travel."

"Jodie's different."

Paul was silent.

"Just don't get your hopes up, Kalvin."

Kalvin didn't answer.

"I'll finish this beer and I'm off to bed."

"OK. Next Juneau we'll party."

"Righto," said Kalvin.

The girls visited the botanical gardens, had a real bus ride on a Canadian bus to a posh restaurant, and visited the zoo, where they saw tigers, bears and zebras. They had their pictures taken and had such fun. It came to an end too quickly as they picked up the taxi to go back to the *Spring Sun*, sad and happy at the same time.

They arrived back at four on the Wednesday. The ship was hot. They were careful where they were treading as they made their way to their various cabins. The laundry was limited to a short time working due to water shortages. The girls' laundry would have to wait.

On Saturday they would need to set up the salon for the next cruise – a three-week one, taking them to the ports they had stopped at on the way up the coast from the Panama Canal. Then it would be the Caribbean run for Jodie until January, and her flight home.

Kalvin caught up with Jodie in the galley. She was sat with the girls. They were chatting over the best times that they'd had during the past three days.

"Back to spaghetti and tomatoes, Allanah."

"Yes, Jodie. Maybe you'll get taken out?"

She saw Kalvin approaching. "Hi there, all," he said.

He came to sit down next to Jodie. She was trying to be interested in her spaghetti.

"Are you eating that?" he asked.

"No, not really."

"Fancy a meal out, then?"

Allanah smiled.

"Yes, I would," she said.

"Meet me on the gangway at seven forty-five. I'll get changed first," said Kalvin, who was in his boiler suit.

She put down her fork and kissed him. "Lovely."

"I'll see you in a while." He hugged Jodie.

"OK."

The ship in dry dock seemed to Jodie, after the few days away, like a shipwreck beached on the sand. She was having some major repairs, painting and mechanical work done.

When Jodie got to the gangway Kalvin was waiting for her, dressed in jeans and a white short-sleeved shirt with trainers. Every time she saw him she had this surge of love for this man. She hurried towards him – she was late. Good job he was a patient person!

"Sorry I'm late. Where are we going?"

"I've been told there's a great restaurant and piano bar on the top floor of a hotel in the middle of Vancouver City, just a taxi ride away."

"That must be the Pacific. It's the tallest building in Vancouver."

"Yes, that's it."

It was a ten-minute ride into the city. They passed bars, shops, people on buses, people busy with their everyday lives. It was a bustling cosmopolitan mix of cultures. The driver stopped just a little way back from the entrance. Jodie got out, followed by Kalvin after he had paid the driver.

Jodie took his arm, then they made their way inside to the lobby, going through a rotating door. The decor inside was quite amazing, including a mural of the Rocky Mountains, with bears and flowing rivers and a canoe paddled by two Indians in the foreground.

They made their way to the lift. The restaurant was on the sixteenth floor. The lift was crowded. Stepping out, they could hear the soft tones of a baby grand piano. People were sitting by the window to see the view of the lights over the city. The waiter took them to an intimate table for two just one row away from the window. It was very romantic.

"Would you care to order wine and see the food menu, ma'am?"

"Yes, please," Jodie said to him.

He gave Jodie and Kalvin the menus.

"I'll have the steak and salad," said Kalvin.

"I'll have the salmon and side salad, please."

"Chardonnay and a beer for me," said Kalvin.

"How was your stay on Vancouver Island, Jodie?"

"Really good, Kalvin – such fun with the girls. We get on so well."

"That's nice. You look better for a rest."

"Thank you. This is lovely here – the lights look so

pretty over the city. Sometimes it's hard to take in just how many places the *Spring Sun* has taken me to in these few short months."

"It's great to see you're enjoying yourself."

"Well, it has to do with present company."

The waiter arrived with their order.

"Fabulous meal."

"Yes, the steak looks great."

"So does the salmon."

Jodie finished her meal and sat back sipping her glass of wine. Kalvin finished just after Jodie. They both were full.

"Better than ship food, Jodie."

"Yes, it was, Kalvin. Shall we sit in the comfy seats?"

"Good idea."

They moved to a sofa by the window. The pianist was playing soft romantic music. A candle was on the table and the lights of Vancouver City shone and sparkled in the distant night sky like stars.

All too soon the evening ended. They were the last people in the restaurant.

"I guess we'd better go," said Kalvin, "or we'll be getting locked in."

"Now, that would be nice."

"Yes, maybe it would."

"Ha ha! We'd miss 'sail away' in a few days' time."

"Best get back. You ready?"

"Yes."

They made their way to the lift and then back to the ship.

Back on the **MS** *Spring Sun* they made their way to Jodie's cabin. There was less disruption there from the repairs, so less noise. Jodie opened the door. They sat down on Jodie's bed and fell into an embrace, slowly enjoying the moments that followed until dawn broke, on another day.

CHAPTER 14

Alaskan Adventures

Skagway was one of the smallest ports on the **MS *Spring Sun***'s route in Alaska – an old gold-mining town that in its heyday was a busy, bustling town where men traded the nuggets they had panned in the river, for food and supplies.

The passengers of the ***Spring Sun*** were given talks on the history of the town. Flightseeing tours were offered to see the glaciers from above, and one afternoon Jodie volunteered to help in exchange for going on a tour.

It left at one for two hours. She saw the passengers on, then sat at the front, ready to see them get off the plane safely.

The pilot's name was Peter. He had lived in Alaska since he was fourteen, when his father, Gerald, married his mother. She was a Native American from Alaska whose name Amitola meant 'Rainbow'.

"Hi there," he said before he took off, sat at the pilot controls. "I'm Peter."

"Hello. I'm Jodie."

"Is everyone on?"

"Yes. I've checked the list and told the passengers to buckle up."

"Great! Take a seat yourself and strap in, then we'll be on our way."

"OK, Peter."

Jodie sat and put her safety belt on.

He clicked the engine into start, the propellers started spinning and then, before they knew it, the little twenty-seater light aeroplane was rising above the runway with its wheels tucked into the undercarriage.

Climbing up into a cloudy but sunny sky, Jodie was feeling elated. Below she could see the **Spring Sun**, the *Canadian Adventurer* and the *Autumn Sun* looking regal, tied up in the dock. They looked so small, like toys on a boating lake. The mountain peaks could be seen ahead.

Peter took a left turn and started commentating over the Tannoy: "You will see to your right the Alaskan mountains. Denali is the highest peak in Alaska, 6,190 metres high. Bordering the Pacific coast. In winter they are impassable. In summer they attract visitors from all over the globe – walkers, climbers, gyrocopters and film crews. They recently filmed *Above the Edge* here, which you may have seen. The principal actors were Michela Dunkirk and Miranda Lomas."

The views were breathtaking. They were so high in the sky it seemed like heaven.

Peter took a right turn, then flew straight between the glaciers, taking them as close as was safe to do so. Jodie looked ahead through the front screen to where a glacier ran. It was a river of frozen ice, and it seemed so close she felt she could almost touch it. The ice, blue, grey, silver and white, was shimmering in the sunshine.

Then they soared up high again to go towards the port, back to the ships and the little runway. As they descended everything came into view.

The tour over, Jodie helped the passengers off, checked the plane for their left-behind belongings then picked up her rucksack, and made her way down the plane steps. Peter was waiting at the bottom.

"Thanks, Peter. I really enjoyed that. The glaciers are spectacular – so amazing."

"Yes, Jodie," he smiled. "Thank you."

Jodie stepped down, the engine quiet now.

"I'm taking a break for the day. The next tour is at two tomorrow. Will you be coming again?" he asked Jodie.

"No, Peter. We can only do one free tour."

"Shame! You were great with the passengers."

She smiled. "Peter, you're a great pilot."

He saluted her, raising his hand to his flying cap, then shut the doors as he climbed out.

Back on board the **MS *Spring Sun*** Jodie went to her cabin to change into her uniform for 'sail away' and the formal night with 'captain's cocktails'. On her way forward she saw Kalvin working on the safety equipment near the lifeboats. He glanced up and waved to Jodie.

She waved back and blew him a kiss, then took a door leading towards a front stairwell.

Slightly exhausted, she opened her cabin door then lay down on her bunk. Not meaning to, she drifted into sleep.

She woke up with a start as there was a knock on the cabin door.

"Jodie, it's Debbie. Are you OK?"

"Oh!"

In a daze Jodie opened the door to her.

"Jodie, we wondered where you were. Jayne's going frantic."

"I'm OK. What's the time?"

"It's nearly six."

"Oh! Crickey, I'm late!"

"OK, I'll wait for you. We'll tell her you had a headache from the flightseeing tour."

Jodie got dressed and took a sip of water.

"We'll get tea on the way up."

"It was so high – probably the altitude made me sleepy. OK, do I look all right, Debbie?"

"Yes – a bit glazed."

"Tea will help."

"Let's go, then, Jodie."

They locked the cabin door and made their way to the crew galley to get tea, then made their way upstairs to the salon at the back of the **Spring Sun**. It was busy. Jodie entered first, followed by Debbie.

"Hello, Jodie. Are you well?" asked Jayne.

"Yes, Jayne. The aeroplane altitude made me a little dizzy earlier."

"Yes, that happens."

"OK, ladies are waiting for formal updos. Get yourself a station, check the equipment and get started, please," she said to Jodie in a direct authoritative fashion.

"Will do, Jayne."

Both girls got on with their tasks, and before they knew it it was 7 p.m. and time to close up.

"OK, all," said Jayne. "Time out! Dinner and crew bar!"

The day came to an end. The girls fell into their beds, and before they knew it another Vancouver day approached. The sun rose and they had docked.

That day Jodie had a letter from home. She opened it.

Dear Jodie,

Everything here is the same as normal. Your brothers are taking me out for a meal to Burley Tea Rooms on Sunday. Thank you for the birthday card. I've put it on the mantelpiece.

Tabatha, the cat, was poorly and had to go to the vet's, but she is getting better now.

I miss you and hope you are well.

All my love,
Mum xx

Jodie folded the letter and put it in the envelope. Then she went to sit on a deckchair, suddenly feeling homesick. She missed home – the lawns, the flowers, birds in the garden, her brothers and sisters, and family parties where they would argue over who was doing the washing-up.

She went to find Kalvin. It was lunchtime, so he'd be in

the crew bar. She needed a big hug. As she walked in, he was sat in his usual spot with the guys, beer can in hand, cheery as ever.

Jodie sat down next to him. All the guys said hi to her; she said hello back. She put her arm in his and asked if he could spare her five minutes.

"Yes, sure." He looked at Jodie. "Are you OK?"

"Hmm!"

"Let's go out on deck."

He got up, she went in front of him and they stepped out into the sunshine.

"I've heard from home, Kalvin."

"Everything OK?"

"Yes, but I feel so homesick."

He looked steadily into her eyes, put his arms around her and held her close, then kissed the top of her head. The tears came then.

"Let it out, Jodie. You know, losing a parent can be something that you hold in."

She sobbed into his shirt.

Tilting Jodie's head, he kissed away her tears, then kissed her mouth. "It's OK," he whispered.

"Thank you, Kalvin."

"You're welcome. Want to go out for a meal in Vancouver next Saturday?"

Jodie, still choking back the sobs: "Yes, that would be lovely."

"Send your mum a postcard, Jodie. Dave, the bar steward, is going home – he'll take it for you and post it in London."

She was quiet. "Yes, good idea."

"Jodie, I have to get back to work."

"Yes, so do I," she said.

Kalvin held her tight and kissed her again.

LIVE EACH DAY

So live each day as if it's your last,
For an angel will guide you along the right path.
When you've always known, and been shown
Open arms to hold you or a voice on the phone.

When you're blue and depressed,
Your friends are far, do not distress.

You know you can go on, for life is like a song.
The note you start with is fresh and full,
The note in the middle a little bit mellow,
But the note at the end, when the song starts to ascend,
Gives you the courage, the will, the knowledge,
To be just you.

by Marion Joy

LOVE

When you've always known, and been shown
Open arms to hold you or a voice on the phone,
Love comes through to every bone.
When you're blue and depressed,
Your friends are far, do not distress.
Love comes through – a letter from home.
You know you can go on, for life is like a song.
The note you start with is fresh and full,
The note in the middle a little bit mellow,
But the note at the end, when the song starts to ascend,
Gives you the courage, the will, the knowledge,
To be just you.
This is when love really shines through.

by Marion Joy

CHAPTER 15

Christmas at Sea, 1985

Jodie felt an emptiness when Kalvin left to go home on leave; despite his reassurance, life on board for her had lost its shine. She spent the first week after he had gone immersing herself in work, writing home and just wanting to be away from people, which on a ship wasn't easy.

They had a new team member, Janet, who was Welsh, a therapist, so Jenny had arranged to give Jodie the job of showing her around and introducing her to the crew. It was three weeks to Christmas. The passenger numbers were up, the salon busy and everyone was working very hard.

Christmas decorations started to appear in the crew bar. In the foyer they had put up the hugest Christmas tree Jodie had ever seen. Decorated with white and gold candles, it had to be chained down so that it wouldn't rock when the **Spring Sun** was going through choppy waters. It looked amazing. Two weeks to Christmas, the Caribbean sun at its hottest, Jodie started to come out of herself again.

Maurice, who to Jodie looked like Captain Bird, had a beard, was balding on top, wore a blue cap and round spectacles and smoked a pipe. Jodie had realised he had been assigned by Kalvin to keep an eye on her. He had invited her, Janet, Allanah and some other close crew members to go ashore in San Juan to the rainforest restaurant. He had a girlfriend in the port who could book a table, arrange a taxi and make it a whole day's adventure. Set for the coming Saturday, Jodie was looking forward to it. They were a jolly lot, full of fun.

Janet, being Welsh, had a wry sense of humour.

At 1 p.m., after the coxswains had done their eight-to-twelve shift, they met by the gangway to be collected by a taxi – or so Jodie thought. Maurice – his jovial self – arrived first, followed by Janet, Trevor and herself.

They walked down the gangway and were greeted at the bottom by a short, lovely Spanish lady called Maralinga, Maurice's girlfriend.

Maurice greeted her with a kiss, held her hand and led the way to the waiting vehicle – Maralinga's wide pink Cadillac. They got in, Maurice in the front seat, the girls in the back with Trevor in the middle.

It was a beautiful tropical sunny day with a few clouds around but none too threatening. They made their way into the city, then took the outbound route to the freeway, which started to climb, winding its way towards mountains. They chatted on the way, Janet and Trevor getting on famously. Jodie chatted to Maralinga about the local area and her life. She was an interesting lady.

There was dense vegetation, but the sunshine was glimpsed through the trees from time to time. The vegetation grew more sparse the higher they got, and at last Maralinga parked the car in an open space. They all got out to look at the view from high above the city – an amazing sight. Leading the way past a small stream, which Maralinga said grew into a huge waterfall, she took them on a path which led to the rainforest restaurant called Santangonas. They could not have found this place without help, for it was tucked away. Maralinga said she had been there many times for family gatherings; she was pleased to take them there that day.

As they entered, the host gave her a huge welcome and kissed her on the cheek, holding her hand, then shook Maurice's hand in turn.

"Come – I have the best seats by the view to the waterfall at the back of the restaurant."

Jodie thought his English was very good.

They followed Sanchez to the table, prepared exquisitely with napkins, coloured glassware and an array of tropical bird of paradise flowers. There was a wonderful view from the terrace of the waterfall and dense vegetation below. It was just stunning. They could hear tropical birds communicating and the sound of running water gushing down to the pool below.

Jodie got out her camera. "Guys, I need a photo to capture the moment."

They gathered round, the picture perfectly capturing the awesome scene behind them.

"Let's eat," said Maurice. "I'm famished."

He put out his pipe, tucked it into his pocket then sat down. Maralinga sat next to him, Janet next to Trevor and Jodie on the other side of Maurice.

They ordered wine – red and white – for the ladies, beers for the guys.

The menu arrived. Sanchez was very attentive.

"May I suggest our dish of the day: lobster and prawn paella with green salad and enchiladas?"

"Sounds fabulous," said Jodie. "Yes, I'll have that."

The others ordered the same.

After the meal they posed outside the restaurant for photos, with the beautiful rainforest as the backdrop.

Maralinga was so happy that her friends had enjoyed themselves. She drove them all back to the *Spring Sun* and kissed Maurice goodbye.

A LASTING FRIENDSHIP

A treasure to behold, clasped hands that unfold,
When asked to be there, no distance too far,
Highest of mountains, strongest of seas,
Rivers and lakes, till I reach thee.
As precious as platinum, as red as a rose,
As bedazzling as a diamond,
Solid as silver, everlasting as an emerald,
A jewel precious as any precious stone.
Past loves, past lives,
Bringing the wisdom that keeps it secure
In our hearts, minds and beliefs,
A lasting friendship that will endure.

by Marion Joy

CHAPTER 16

The Homecoming

As flight 257 from Miami to London touched down, Jodie was glad to be on terra firma. She sat and waited until the plane had come to a standstill, then opened her eyes. She found flying claustrophobic and knew she could not get used to it.

The aeroplane window showed it had been snowing. Gatwick airport in midwinter looked bleak and uninviting. She was dressed in a long cotton pencil skirt, black high heels and red boxy jacket with a thin blouse underneath. Tanned from head to toe, she had thick layered mid-length blonde hair. That morning she had been sunning herself on the rooftop terrace at the Haliday Inn. She wished she had brought a jumper at least.

Kalvin had promised to meet her, she had sent her flight details by post as soon as she had been given them a week ago. The plane had been delayed at Miami due to the bad weather in England. Jodie made her way to customs and checked through, her luggage would follow, she was told.

As she went through the final gate she saw him. He wore a blue shirt, faded blue jeans and a brown fleece flying jacket with trainers. He smiled a broad grin, his deep-brown eyes looking back at her with a solid look. He looked just the same as when she saw him four weeks ago, when he went home on leave from the *Spring Sun* and the Caribbean, except his tan had faded.

They held each other so tight for at least five minutes.

Then he said, "Great to see you again! Did you have a good flight?"

"I missed you, Kalvin. The flight was OK, but I'm freezing."

"I brought a spare coat for you, Jodie."

"Thank you."

"We'll pick up your luggage and then we'll go. The car's parked nearby."

He took her case and picked up the larger one from the carousel, then they walked hand in hand to the car. Jodie was shivering. He held her again, then kissed her – a long, slow kiss that made her forget she was cold at all.

"Hop in, then," he said as he opened the door. He went around to the rear and put the luggage in the car.

"Thank you – so good to see you again."

"I'll put the heater on. Put the coat around your shoulders, Jodie. Mum's making lunch – sausage and mash – then I'm sure you'll want a lie-down. Jet lag will catch up with you very soon."

"OK. I'm looking forward to meeting your folks."

As he drove, Jodie could appreciate what he had written about Romney Marsh being so flat, even though the land and hedgerows were covered in snow, she could make out the sheep's sort of shadowy shapes.

She listened to the music – 'The Power of Being Loved'. It was so appropriate. Kalvin was his usual relaxed self. They had been living together on the ship **MS *Spring Sun*** for six months, apart from four weeks while Jodie's contract finished and Kalvin had gone home on leave.

She was a little nervous about meeting his parents, northern folk from Newcastle upon Tyne – a place Jodie had only seen on the TV and on maps. She had also never been to Kent. She wondered what he had said to his parents about her.

About twenty minutes later, he came to a stop outside some houses. Everything was white. It was a narrow street. There was a snow-covered wooden gate, and a small garden with a path cleared of snow to a blue front door.

"Here we are – this is home for me, Jodie."

He turned off the car engine, got out, then came around to the passenger side and opened the car door for her.

She stepped out and pulled the coat he had given her around her shoulders. It was freezing! She felt goosebumps on her bare legs.

"Let's get you inside and get the kettle on. I'll bring your luggage in from the car."

"Kalvin, I'm nervous. Will they like me OK?"

He smiled. "You're all right – they won't bite!"

She gave him a quizzical look, he squeezed her hand to reassure her.

The Wheelers lived in a two-bedroom first-floor flat. It was tiny compared to her mum's three-bedroom council house and garden. It was, as Jodie entered the lounge, full of pictures on the wall, warm, cosy and welcoming.

His mum, Sylvia, came towards her and put her arms around her. "Reggie and I have heard so much about you from Kalvin, glad to finally meet you."

Sylvia, a mere four-foot-eight, brunette, blue eyes and a northern accent, had, Kalvin said, been looking forward to meeting her. Jodie breathed a sigh of relief.

"Let's get the kettle on and we'll chat until lunch is ready."

Jodie smiled and Kalvin's dad, Reggie, smiled back. He had Kalvin's broad looks and smile. He was sitting in a cosy armchair.

"Kalvin's been that nervous about your flight coming in on time – he was heading to the airport for 9 a.m. today. I told him to wait a bit, just as well as it was a late arrival."

"Thank you for making me feel at home," Jodie added. "Kalvin's told me so much about you, I feel I know you already. Sorry if I seem a bit vague – it's been a long day already."

The front door went click as Kalvin came in after parking the car. He appeared and came to sit next to her on the little green sofa.

"Good to see you've all got along," he said.

Kalvin's dad grinned. "We've not eaten her alive!"

Just then Kalvin's mum came in from the kitchen carrying a tray of tea and cakes. "Tea up, all!"

"Just what I needed – I wasn't dressed for the cold English climate! Great tea, Sylvia."

"Thanks, love."

Jodie noticed Kalvin was aloof in front of his folks. She had so missed him.

Kalvin was so happy inside to see Jodie again. It had seemed so very long, and now she was here. He was nervous, but all seemed good between his parents and Jodie – the first girl he'd brought home. She was so special to him.

They all chatted for a while, and then sat at the table for a lovely lunch: beef sausages, mashed spuds, also Yorkshire puds and veg, just as Kalvin had said. It was delicious – especially the taties as Kalvin's dad called them – washed down with a glass of red wine.

Jodie could feel herself flagging, she was stuffed and a bit tipsy. She was sat across the table from Sylvia. Kalvin and his dad were at opposite ends.

"Sylvia, that was a fab meal. Food on board wasn't bad, but Kalvin and I would eat out when in port. America doesn't do Yorkshire puds!"

Sylvia laughed. "That's what Kalvin says."

"Kalvin, can I go and lie down for an hour? Hope you don't mind, Sylvia?"

"You go in Kalvin's room and take a nap. Make yourself at home."

"Thank you."

Jodie slipped off her shoes and laid down her weary head, and as she drifted off to sleep she sensed a feeling of calm come over her.

Kalvin came in to join her, he held her close, "Stay with me always Jodie."

Her dreams were of the **MS *Spring Sun***, life on board, the places she had visited. Kalvin's strong, warm, embrace under the stars of boat deck, with the sound of the sea, lost in the magic of his lips meeting hers, in their first kiss.